BEN BOVA & GORDON R. DICKSON

GREMLINS GO HOME

A JIM BAEN PRESENTATION

TOR

A TOM DOHERTY ASSOCIATES BOOK

GREMLINS GO HOME

Copyright ©1983 by Ben Bova and Gordon Dickson

A TOR Book

Published by:

Tom Doherty Associates, Inc.
8-10 West 36th Street
New York, New York 10018

First TOR printing, November 1983

ISBN: 812-53-221-X
CAN. ED. 812-53-222-8

Cover art by Tom Kidd

Interior illustrations by Kelly Freas

Printed in the United States of America

Distributed by:
Pinnacle Books
1430 Broadway
New York, New York 10018

GREMLINS GO HOME

1

It was a week before the Mars launch.

THE launch, everybody was calling it around Cape Kennedy.

Big deal! thought Rolf Gunnarson as he opened the garage door. The door slipped out of his hands and rattled noisily up on its tracks, slamming against the end of the tracks with a loud *thump*! For a moment Rolf winced, thinking the noise would wake his baby sister, then he set his jaw. Let it!

Rolf squeezed past his father's white official NASA car to get to his old three-speed bicycle. *So, I don't need a ten-speed, do I?* he muttered to himself. *He's just too busy with his space shot to listen to me. I really need that bike to get back and forth to the Wildlife Refuge. But he doesn't care about the ecology, the Refuge, or anything — except being Launch Director for this Mars flight!*

His face set in an unhappy scowl, Rolf wheeled the three-speed out of the garage and through the half-dozen cars parked along the driveway. Out on the street a big TV truck was parked. Inside the house the TV men were laying cables and setting up lights and cameras. They were going to interview his father. THE launch was only a few days away.

"You'd think he was one of them — one of the astronauts going to Mars," Rolf said to Shep, who was lying in the shade of the orange tree in the Gunnarsons' front yard. Shep looked like a ball of brown and white wool with a red tongue hanging out.

It was as hot a day as Florida can produce in August. The sun blazed out of a brilliant blue sky that was flecked here and there with gleaming white, puffy clouds. But Rolf couldn't hang around the house any longer. First it was his father telling him, "Not now, Rolf! Can't you see I'm busy? After THE launch we'll talk about it." Then it was the TV crew bustling around the house, saying, "Hey kid, wouldya mind gettin' outta the way?"

Rolf whistled for Shep to come along, and started pedaling for the Merritt Island National Wildlife Refuge. He had been going to stay home from it today. But now . . .

"I should've brought some lemonade or something," he told himself as he pumped along the street, passing the neat little houses with their lawns and flowering bushes and trees.

For a moment he thought about going back, but then he shook his head. *Maybe I'll never go back,* he thought grimly, as he turned off the street and headed for the Old Courtney Pike.

He rode for several miles in silence, with Shep scampering along beside him. Hot as it was, the speed of his travel put a breeze in his face and set his unbuttoned shirt flapping loosely behind him, so that he felt the air slipping over his bare chest, blowing out the armholes of his sleeves, like his own personal air conditioner. *Just like the astronauts,* he thought, picturing in his mind how they must feel inside their air-conditioned space suits.

Riding the bike felt good—even in the heat. Not that any kind of heat could bother Rolf, really. He was used to it. Just like old Shep, looking as woolly as any other English sheepdog anywhere in the world, trotting along beside the bicycle with his red tongue hanging out. Anybody who didn't know better would think Shep was ready to melt. But Rolf knew the sheepdog could keep up with him like this all day. They were both Floridians born and bred. Shep would guess they were headed toward the Wildlife Refuge, a place he liked as well as Rolf did.

Most people didn't even realize that the Refuge existed. All they cared about, like Rolf's dad, was the Space Center part of Cape Kennedy. Actually, the Refuge was almost 85,000 acres in size. That was about ninety-nine percent of all the land the Space Agency owned on the Cape. The launching Center took up the remaining one percent. The Refuge was a haven for birds. Officially there were 224 different species of birds visiting there regularly—although Rolf himself had checked off 284 species last year. And there were the permanent residents, too; tough wild pigs, snakes, bald eagles and even alligators. A good place to get away to, when things at home got to the point where you wanted to kick holes in the wall.

Right now, however, the desire to kick holes in the wall was diminishing in him. As usual, the exercise of the ride and the prospect of getting back to the Refuge were working their good influence on him. Now that he was beginning to feel better, Rolf admitted to himself that it was not really things like not having a ten-speed bike that were bothering him. It was . . . he could not seem to say what it was. Sometimes, when he was away from home, like this, he would make up his mind not to let things get to him when he went home again. But they always did. Or at least, since this summer started, they always did. Remembering the past weeks, Rolf scowled again. Summer vacation was supposed to be something you looked forward to. But nothing seemed to have gone right this year—from his slipping off the diving board and hurting his leg, right up until now. First there had been that accident, then the upset of the house after his baby sister was born. Now THE launch . . .

Busy thinking, he reached the edge of the Refuge almost before he knew it. But then, suddenly, the road was in among the acres of wild land, and he looked around himself feeling good. Most people might have seen nothing much to enjoy. There were only sandy little hillocks covered with coarse grass and scrubby brush, in all directions, with an occasional bigger tree pushing crookedly higher against the glittering sky. But to Rolf it was a remarkable and fascinating place, busy with plant, bird and animal life, all of which were particular friends of his. From the wild sow with her four piglets right now trotting along in plain sight beside the road he was riding, to a brown hen pelican, nesting in a secret pool he knew of, far out among the brush—and who already had lost one of her three eggs because of the thinness of its shell, due to DDT—they were individuals with whom he was concerned.

The sow led her family off back into the brush, and a little farther on Rolf turned his bike from the concrete highway onto the asphalt road that led down in the direction of the Playalinda Beach part of the Refuge. Then, a short distance down the asphalt, he cut off the road entirely and bumped along on one of the old foot trails that wound through the Preserve.

Officially, no one was supposed to be here, right now. That was why he had not planned to come today. Playalinda Beach was officially closed when there was a rocket on the pad at LC-39, as the Mars rocket stood right now.

But who cared? All that the Beach's being closed meant was that nobody else would be around. *And who wants anybody else around?* Rolf asked himself. *It's good to be alone. Nobody here except me and Shep.*

Shep?

Rolf suddenly realized that Shep was no longer trotting beside his bike. By itself that wasn't so odd, since the trail was too narrow in spots to let the bike and the dog go side by side. But in that case, Shep should be right behind him. Rolf glanced back, squinting against the glaring sunshine.

Shep was behind him, all right. But a long way behind. The sheepdog was sitting at the last bend of the trail they had passed, some fifty yards behind Rolf, gazing at him disapprovingly. Rolf braked the bike and stopped. He put his feet down on the sandy ground and half turned around.

"Come on!" yelled. "Shep! Come on!"

Shep didn't move. But he barked—which complicated matters.

Shep wasn't like other dogs, in a number of ways. One of these was the way he barked. He had a gruff voice, to begin with, but there was more to it than that. When most dogs bark they seem to be saying, "Hey, glad to see you!" or "Look out! Warning! Stand back!"

Shep's bark was more like the shout of an angry old gentlemen telling someone to mind his manners. "About time you got here," Shep would seem to say. Or, "Stop that nonsense immediately."

"Rrarhf!" said Shep now. It was exactly as if he had snapped, "Get back here at once!"

"Shep," said Rolf slowly, "I'm in no mood for that today. Do you hear me?"

"Huroof!" said Shep.

"What's wrong with you, anyway?"

"Rharf! Rharf rharuff!"

"Listen, I'm going down this trail whether you like it or not."

"Rruff!"

"Then I'll go by myself!"

"Rrarhr!"

15

"Suit yourself," said Rolf, turning around and getting the bike started again. "Just go on and suit yourself!"

He rode off. After a few minutes, and a couple of bends of the trail, he caught a flicker of movement out of the corner of his eye and glanced down to see Shep once more pacing beside him.

"Mrrmp," muttered Shep darkly, deep in his woolly throat. But he kept moving alongside the bike. Rolf felt a small twinge of guilt.

"I do things you want to do sometimes, don't I?" Rolf demanded.

Shep was silent now. He trotted along with his black nose in the air. Rolf shrugged and gave up. Shep's reluctance to go down the trail was making Rolf all the more curious to see where it led. He must have been down this trail before, because he had roamed all over the trails in the Playalinda Beach area at one time or another. But just now he couldn't remember when, or which way this particular trail led.

They were mounting a small rise to a sandy top. Nothing could be seen beyond the top of the rise except the hot blue sky. Under Rolf's hard-pumping legs, the bicycle mounted to the crest and then pitched steeply down into a long dip.

Never saw this spot before! Rolf thought. And it was just as the bike nosed down-

ward that Shep reached up, clamped his teeth firmly on the ragged edge of the cut-off jeans just above Rolf's knee, and dug all four paws solidly into the ground, putting on the brakes.

It was Rolf's weak leg, the one he had hurt at the pool. The bike skidded wildly, crosswise off the path and started to fall over. Even so, it shouldn't have fallen all the way, since Rolf was an experienced rider. He stuck out his leg to prop up the bike and stop the fall.

But his foot slipped on the sandy soil, his

leg buckled, the bike fell, and Rolf went tumbling down the rest of the slope to the bottom of the dip.

"Shep!" he yelled — or tried to yell. Oddly, his voice came out as a small squeak. Furious, Rolf tried to sit up, but he didn't make it even halfway. The dip around him seemed to fill up with a pearly white mist. It was impossible for him to see anything an arm's length away. His head buzzed with a wild dizziness that made it feel as though he were spinning madly.

Rolf collapsed back onto the sand and everything blanked out.

2

Rolf gradually drifted back to consciousness.

The hot brilliance of the sun made everything seem red through his closed eyelids. Slowly, the buzz in his head eased off, and in its place he could hear two voices arguing. One voice was very deep-toned and very British in accent. The other was a high-pitched, very Irish tenor.

" . . . beastly fellows!" the deep voice was snorting.

"Ah, there you go again now," retorted the Irish-sounding voice. "Don't you know there's no one speaks like that, these days? Indeed, it's exactly like Dr. Watson with Sherlock Holmes, you sound, and out of a hundred years ago."

"Well you *are* beastly fellows," growled the other voice. "Pack of blackguards! Besides, what d'you mean—talk like a hundred years ago? Speak like any well-brought-up individual of good breeding, if I say it myself."

"That you don't," said the Irish voice, teasingly, "as I've no doubt you well know. It's an entirely artificial way of speech you've got there, copied out of th' late movies you've been watchin' on the TV . . . *yikes!*"

The deep voice growled again, but this time it was a real growl.

"Now, now—no need to be hasty," cried the Irish voice, suddenly seeming to come from a position higher up. "Indeed, no offense meant. None whatsoever, Mr. Shepterton."

Rolf cracked an eyelid open to see what was going on. And immediately wished he hadn't.

He saw Shep, with bared teeth and curled upper lip, staring up at a small bush. Floating slightly above the bush, in midair, was an impossible little man no more than a foot tall, with large pointed ears and big white eyebrows, like wings. He was dressed in a close-fitting, long-sleeved green jacket and tight green pants that ended in small black boots with pointed, curled toes.

And Shep was talking? "TV? Blasted impertinence! Talk the way I do because I am

what I am. What if it's a bit old-fashioned?
No harm in that."

"None whatsoever, Mr. Sheperton. None
at all!" said the little man, still floating above
the bush. "It's a darling way of speaking you

have, indeed it is, when all's said and done.
And if they speak the same way in old movies
on the TV, now, why sure it must be that
they're trying to catch the proper grand manner of speech belonging to gentlemen such
as yourself."

Shep backed off from the bush. His lip
uncurled.

Rolf closed his eyes again. It couldn't be—what he thought he was seeing and hearing. Shep talking like a human being and a little man in green answering him? He must have hit his head on a rock when he fell off the bike. . . . There, the voices had stopped. No doubt when he opened his eyes again he would see no one but good old Shep whining like an ordinary dog and trying to lick his face.

But—

"Let's put it out of mind then," said the Irish voice, quite clearly. "Sure and we've much more important matters to discuss, haven't we now?"

Rolf opened both eyes this time. The little man was floating down to the ground at the foot of the bush. Shep had seated himself on his haunches.

"If you mean the boy," Shep said gruffly, "there's nothing for us to discuss. He's my ward, you know. I'll not have him associating with blackguards, will-o-the-wisps—*or* gremlins. And it's a gremlin that you are, in spite of your green suit and green accent. . . . Speaking of the way *I* talk, how about you?"

"Now Mr. Sheperton, now," said the gremlin, or whatever he was, soothingly. "Let's not dig up old bones to pick. . . . "

"Don't know why not," muttered Shep—or Mr. Sheperton, as the gremlin called him. "Many a happy hour I've spent digging . . ."

"I meant only that there's no need for us to argue further on the matter of speech," said the gremlin. "It's the boy we should be talking about. A fine lad—"

"Naturally. Educated him myself," said Mr. Sheperton.

"And indeed it shows. Indeed it does," said the gremlin hastily. "But the point is, the lad's been troubled—there's no denying that."

"Life's not a bed of roses," gruffed Mr. Sheperton. "Have to take the rough with the smooth."

"To be sure. But why take the rough at all, if you may go smooth all the way 'round?"

"Builds character, that's why!" snapped Mr. Sheperton. "See here—whatever you call yourself nowadays—"

"Baneen," said the gremlin.

"See here, Baneen. These are human matters. You keep your gremlin nose out of them!" Mr. Sheperton went on. "The boy's had a rough summer. All this interest of his in wild animals made him feel different from his friends to begin with. Then, when he tried to get social again, early this summer, he had the bad luck to crack his leg going off a diving board—showing off, of course, but what's the harm in that—and had to spend several weeks in a cast. Mother busy with an infant sister. Father all tied up with his work. Left him feeling all on his own, just when he got all involved in this ecology business and wanted to start doing something with his life. Very well. He'll work his way through his problems one way or another, and I'll thank you not to interfere."

"*You'll* thank me?" piped Baneen, skipping sideways a few steps before Mr. Sheperton's nose, dancelike on the curled toes of his boots. "Thank me, will you, now? And if I'm not to interfere, what is it yourself is doing?"

"I'm one of the family," growled Mr. Sheperton. "All the difference in the world."

"Ah, indeed? Indeed? And does that give you the right to keep the boy from even considering all the fine help I could be offering?" Rolf's eyes opened wider at this. "Why, a touch, merely a touch of gremlin magic, and he'll find the answer to all his problems and dreams at once. All that in return for just a wee bit of help, hardly the liftin' of his littlest finger . . ."

Mr. Sheperton growled and got to all four legs. Baneen leaped backwards a half step and then started to rise right off the ground. But they were both frozen in their places by a sudden roaring voice:

"BANEEN! AND WHAT ARE YOU UP TO NOW, ME SLIPPERY LITTLE MAN?" Another gremlin stepped from behind a bush. "What's going on here?" he demanded "And who are you, dog?"

"Sheperton. Mr. Sheperton," replied Shep, coldly.

Baneen glided back to the ground and touched down lightly. "Ah there, Lugh, darling," Baneen said, keeping one eye on Shep. "Sure and all, the grim beast would have killed me five times over if it'd not been for your mighty self coming to my rescue. . . ."

"Rescue is it? That depends on what it is that you've been up to," snapped the second gremlin. "Now answer me quick, or I'll be putting you under a spell in a damp cellar for five thousand years—and well, you know I can do it! That or anything else I've a mind to!"

Lying there watching them, Rolf believed the newcomer wholeheartedly. There was something about this gremlin named Lugh that was extremely convincing, although at the same time it was puzzling. Because in an odd way, Lugh seemed to be many times larger and more threatening than he actually was. Rolf squinted at him, wondering if the fall from his bike hadn't done something to his head, after all.

Plainly to view, Lugh was another gremlin like Baneen. Well, not exactly like Baneen. Lugh was half again as tall, wide-shouldered and burly. But it wasn't this alone that made him so impressive—and he *was* impressive indeed.

Somehow, although Rolf's eyes insisted

that Lugh was no more than a foot and a half tall, some inner sense saw it differently. Lugh somehow gave the impression of being the size of a professional football player, massive, heavy-jawed, hard-fisted and more than a match for anything on two legs or four.

"Did you hear me, little man?" roared Lugh now, waving a fist under Baneen's nose. "Speak up, or it's down with you to the toads and mushrooms for five thousand years!"

"Whush now," said Baneen, with a slight quaver in his voice. "It's a terrible temper you have, indeed it is. And me only trying to do a bit of good for man, gremlin and beast alike. Ah, the hard misunderstandings that have been the lot of my life! The misunderstandings of those for whom I wished to do the poor best that I could . . ."

"Talk!" said Lugh fiercely.

"And aren't I, after doing that very thing, this moment?" Baneen said quickly. "As my tongue was just now saying, here was I in talk with Mr. Sheperton. . . ."

"Mr. Sheperton?" Lugh blinked, then turned to look at the dog. "Oh yes—Sheperton."

"*Mr.* Sheperton, if you don't mind!" Shep growled dangerously.

"Now, now, let's not be having a misunderstanding," said Baneen hastily, stepping between the sheepdog and Lugh. "Mr.

Sheperton it is, indeed—so named by the family of the lad when they brought him home as a wee pup, nearly six long years ago."

Rolf blinked. Slowly, out of far back in his mind, swam up a memory of the day when his father had brought the dog into their house. It was true—the first name they had given to the fuzzy, wobbly-legged puppy stumbling over the kitchen floor had been "Mr. Sheperton." The name had been given because there was something pompous about the plump waddling puppy, even then. Of course, the original name was soon forgotten and shortened to "Shep."

"—and may I present now," Baneen was going on, "himself, Lugh of the Long Hand, Prince of all Gremlins on this chill and watery planet of yours, second to none but His Royal Majesty the King of Gremla Itself—long may its bright clouds of dust blow against the sunset."

Baneen wound up this short speech by blowing his nose sentimentally.

Mr. Sheperton and Lugh grunted ungraciously at each other in acknowledgement of the introduction.

"Prince I am, and don't you forget it," said Lugh, shaking his fist once more at Baneen. "If there's to be any dealings with human beings, I'll be the one to do them. That's understood?"

"To be sure, to be sure," Baneen soothed. "How could you think I'd go and forget such a thing? I was only preparing the matter for your royal attention—it was nothing more than that I had in mind. Why, says I to myself, here's a boy with troubles that a small touch of gremlin magic can mend, a noble dog to be assisted in his wardship of his—"

"Assisted? Who said I needed assistance?" gruffed Mr. Sheperton.

"No one. No one at all, at all. It was only a figure of speech I was making," Baneen went on. "And here we are, exiles from the planet of our birth, the beautiful and dry Gremla, longing for a way to get back to its lovely, dusty caves. Why not put it all together, thought I, and with the noble Lugh of the Long Hand—the darling of all Gremla that was—to oversee, sure the end can be nothing but happiness for all concerned."

"Get to the point, Baneen-og," rumbled Lugh. "You're reaching an end to the tether of my patience."

"There's no more than a word to be said," Baneen answered quickly. "Here we are marooned these thousands of years on this watery planet where the best of gremlin magic can lift us no more than a dozen feet into the air. And over there—" Baneen pointed in the direction of LC-39, "—is a fine big rocket about to go all the way to Mars, next door to

Gremla so it is, and here is a boy whose father's work is all with that very rocket—"

A bellow from Lugh stopped him. The large gremlin had glanced at Rolf when he was mentioned by Baneen, and—too late—Rolf had realized that he was lying there propped up on his elbows, his eyes wide open.

"BY THE GREAT CAIRNGORM OF GREMLA ITSELF!" Lugh roared, striding wrathfully toward Rolf and seeming to grow more gigantic with each step. "You've sprinkled the lad over with Gremla-dust, Baneen—and that with no permission from anyone, least of all myself! He's been lying here with his eyes open all this time, seeing and hearing and *understanding* every word ourselves and the dog have spoken!"

3

"Lugh!" yelped Baneen. "You overgrown, great—"

Lugh spun around to face the smaller gremlin, and Baneen's tone changed abruptly, sweetly, "—man of wisdom that you are, now. Surely yourself has figured out that the lad must be able to talk with us and see us, if he's to be the means of aiding our poor friend O'Rigami in his and our time of need."

Lugh, who looked as if he had just been about to leap at Baneen, settled back, frowning, and stroked his chin whiskers.

"Oh?" he said thoughtfully. "O'Rigami, is it now?"

"Who else, and what else would it be?

Ah, I see it's yourself has it all figured out already. Here we are, out of the goodness of our green gremlin hearts—"

Mr. Sheperton snorted.

"—the goodness of our hearts, I was saying," Baneen went on blandly, "about to help this lad in his troubles. What more likely, I can see you're thinking, than he'd wish to do us a small favor in return? Sure, and it'd be no more than a second's effort for a bright lad such as himself who's not bothered by cold iron and all the hard things men put about to bar out the likes of us."

"Ah. Hmm . . ." Lugh turned back to scowl thoughtfully at Rolf.

"Come, Lugh!" cried Baneen. "Surely you've got a smile for the young man, after your fearsome looks of a moment ago."

"A . . . smile . . ." muttered Lugh. He made an effort to smile at Rolf. It was about as effective as if a bulldog had tried to simper.

Mr. Sheperton either cleared his throat or growled. It was hard to tell which. "'Ware the gremlin bearing promises," he muttered. "If the Trojans had listened to that advice, they'd have never let that horse inside their gates. . . .

"Just a minute," Rolf said. He sat up and crossed his legs. He was feeling braver now than he had a few minutes before. Not because of Lugh's smile—a tiger would not have felt much braver after having been smiled at by Lugh—but because something Baneen had said was ringing in his ears. Baneen had hinted that there was something that he, Rolf, could do that not all the gremlins with their obviously magical powers, could do. Rolf wanted to learn just what it was.

"Go on, Baneen," he said. "The least I can do is listen."

"Said the fly to the spider," growled Mr. Sheperton.

"Now, now, it's no spider I am at all!" Baneen snapped. "A wee wisp of a gremlin, that's all, far from the golden sands and stinging winds of my native home, helpless on a stranger shore. And so are we all, young Rolf. Indeed, all the gremlins in exile on watery Earth now cast themselves on your mercy. Only you, Rolf Gunnarson, whose name shall ring down the halls of human and gremlin history (if you so choose) can change the course of fate for men and gremlins and bring us safely back to Gremla."

Rolf's ears grew uncomfortably warm. The little man's grandiloquent words were a bit hard to take. He did not appear to be deliberately making fun of Rolf, but Rolf had become sensitive these last couple of years to what people said to him.

"That's a lot for some stranger to be doing for you, isn't it?" Rolf asked. "After all, I never even heard of your Gremla. In fact,

dressed the way you are and everything you two look to me more like—what's the word for them?—leprechauns."

"Well, well, no doubt we do. But what's the matter to that?" said Baneen. "What's in a name? Sure, and if some people want to call us leprechauns, there's no harm done."

"You mean you really are gremlins, but you were just being *called* leprechauns?" demanded Rolf. "But how come then you speak with an Irish accent?"

"Irish accent, indeed!" cried Baneen. "Why, it's a pure and natural gremlin accent you're hearing from hundreds of thousands of years before Ireland rose from the sea. Is it our fault now that the Irish, folk with the fine, musical ear that they have, happened to pick it up from us? In truth, there's no such thing as an Irish accent—it's a gremlin accent you're hearing from them and us alike."

"Likely story!" grumphed Mr. Sheperton. "Rolf—"

"Well, it doesn't matter," said Rolf, quickly before the dog could get started again. "Baneen, you were saying you need help? What is it? What could I do for you?"

"Ah, it's free us from this prison world, you can," Baneen answered. "Set us on our way to home. Oh, to see fair Gremla just once again before . . . before . . ."

He broke down and apparently was unable to go on.

"Why, the dissembling jackanapes!" sputtered Mr. Sheperton. "Rolf, don't be misled and befooled. Like all gremlins, he's immortal. He could spend the next million years here and still go back to his Gremla, fresh as a daisy."

"That's right, now!" said Baneen, weeping openly now and wiping his eyes with his bushy eyebrows. "Reproach me with it, that I'm not mortal. Does that mean that I've no feelings?"

"You hear that, Shep?" said Rolf, embarrassed.

"As long as we're speaking to each other," the dog replied, with great dignity, "I'd prefer that you addressed me by my proper name: Mr. Sheperton."

But Rolf was already saying, "Go on, Baneen. Pay no attention to him. What can I do for you? Anything reasonable I'll be glad to do. Do you need something special so you can get back to Gremla?"

"Well now," said Baneen, suddenly dry-eyed again. "It's a mere handful of something or other we're after needing. Indeed, I don't even know the names of the little things, myself. But I can take you to one who does. The Grand Engineer he is, for our return to Gremla. His name's O'Rigami."

"O'Rigami?" echoed Rolf. The sound of the name was oddly familiar.

"Indeed, that's his very self," Baneen said.

"He's that busy a man he can't be coming here to meet you. But if you'll permit me to weave a wee bit of a spell so's you can enter our Gremlin Hollow . . ."

Baneen's fingers were already making strange fluttering passes in the air. Mr. Sheperton began something that might have been the growl of a warning, but it was cut off almost immediately.

Rolf found himself wrapped in a pale yellow glow, like a faintly luminous fog, and gently lifted to his feet by unseen hands. He walked—without consciously directing his feet—further down the path where he had fallen. The ground seemed to go down and down; the wind from the nearby ocean was absolutely still and silent. But all around him, just beyond the fringes of his fog-shrouded vision, Rolf could hear tiny buzzings and murmurings, and an occasionally high-pitched squeaky laugh.

Then the fog seemed to lift a bit, and he saw at his feet another gremlin. He was sitting cross-legged on the sand, head bent over his work. His hands were moving rapidly.

Rolf got down on his knees to see what the gremlin was doing. His tiny fingers were moving with furious speed. But as far as Rolf could see there was nothing in the gremlin's hands. Nothing at all.

The gremlin looked up and saw Rolf watching him. He bowed his head deeply.

"Ah, sssooo!" he hissed.

Rolf blinked. This gremlin was as small as Baneen, and even slimmer. He wore a white smock over his green suit and his fingers were extraordinarily long, delicate and supple. They kept moving incredibly fast.

The fog was lifting even more, and beyond the busy gremlin Rolf could see dozens of others swarming about an object that looked —no, it couldn't be. But it was. A kite. A huge paper kite.

Something was happening to Rolf's sense of vision, as far as its real size went. Rolf's eyes and his mind were battling over how large the kite really was. To his eyes, it looked like a regular kite, the kind Rolf himself flew at the beach, but Rolf's mind kept insisting that the kite was as big as a jet airliner. And indeed, there seemed to be room enough on it for hundreds of gremlins. Maybe thousands. Or even more.

He shook his head, as if to clear it.

"Wercome to my modest assembry center," said the white-smocked gremlin.

"Eh . . . hello," Rolf stammered. "You're a gremlin too?"

"Of course! Born and bred on Gremra five-point-three thousands of centuries ago. That is, Earth centuries, of course. The year of Gremra is much different from your own."

"Oh . . . yeah." Rolf felt a bit dazed. "But

. . . it's just that—uh—you don't seem to talk with the right accent. . . . "

"*Hai!*" The little gremlin jumped to his feet. "My humbre accent is that of true gremrin attempting to speak your ranguage."

"It sounds Japanese."

"Not so! Honorable Japanese race have acquired accent from gremrins riving amongst them."

"But . . . " Rolf was getting totally confused. "I thought gremlins all talked with an Irish accent, and the Irish . . . "

"Beg to differ . . . "

There was a sudden pop—about as loud as the pop of a cork from a toy gun—and Baneen suddenly appeared beside them.

"Now, now, Rolf me bucko! This is no time to be bothering with trifles of tongue and tone. There's too much to be done!"

Rolf blinked at him.

"Rolf Gunnarson," Baneen went on, without even taking a breath, "may I introduce you to the Great Grand Engineer of All Gremla in Exile—O'Rigami."

O'Rigami hissed and bowed.

Rolf found himself bowing too, even though he was still sitting on his heels on the sand floor of the Gremlin Hollow.

"A small token of my esteem," O'Rigami said gently. His right hand flickered out. For one astonished moment, Rolf could have sworn that the hand and the arms to which it was attached stretched several feet across the sand to where the other gremlins were working on the kite. Within an eyeblink, O'Rigami's hand and arm had returned to normal, but now there was a small square of paper in front of him.

The square of paper seemed to disappear as O'Rigami's amazing fingers quickly folded it into the shape of a beautiful, tiny swan with outstretched wings. The gremlin held it out in his palm, and the miniature paper swan suddenly fluttered its wings and took off. It flew in a circle around Rolf's head before coming down to land with the lightest of touches on his shoulder.

"A memento in honor of our meeting," O'Rigami said, bowing again.

"That's the neatest thing I ever saw!" Rolf said. He picked the swan from his shoulder and held it in his palm. But it wouldn't fly again; it simply sat there, lovely but unmoving. "How'd you do it?"

"Now that's a question would take too long to answer," said Baneen, at his elbow. "But it's a great and wonderful art, so it is."

O'Rigami lifted a hand modestly. "Merely the apprication of sound techniques of construction," he said, "together with the proper magic formuras."

"It's O'Rigami," said Baneen to Rolf, "who is in charge of constructing the craft which will carry us all safely back to Gremla—with

the help of your rocket, of course."

Rolf turned to stare at the gremlin work-men again. "It looks like a kite. . . . "

"And what else would it be, indeed!" said Baneen. "One of the wondrous, great space-going kites of mighty Gremla, such as have explored the very depths of the universe, sailing before the proud winds of Gremlin magic in free space unhampered by any nasty dampness. In such a kite, that very one there, will we return to Gremla—that is, if all goes well—attached to your rocket."

He coughed self-consciously.

"But it's pretty big—I mean," Rolf tried

to think of some way of putting it that wouldn't hurt their feelings. "I don't think something that size can be attached to the Mars rocket without making it fly crooked — I mean, even if the launch crew didn't see it attached to the rocket."

"Of course, now, they won't be seeing it," said Baneen severely. "It'll be invisible. And as for size, that's no problem either. Haven't we O'Rigami himself here to fold it so cleverly it'll seem to be no larger than your hand?"

"Fold?" Rolf stared from Baneen to O'Rigami, who once again politely hissed and bowed. Suddenly Rolf's mind made the connection it had been trying to make ever since he had heard Baneen first pronounce the other gremlin's name. "O'Rigami? Of course! *Origami* — I knew I'd heard about it in school! It's the Japanese art of folding paper. You mean he's learned this Japanese way of folding things so well that he . . ."

O'Rigami shut his eyes and turned his head away.

"Now, now, *now!*" cried Baneen, each word a note higher than the one before it. "Watch your tongue, lad, before you stumble upon an insult and break everything! Is it likely that a gremlin would be needing to learn anything from humans like yourself, who've merely been around for fifty thousand years or so? And O'Rigami himself a respectable half-million in age and more? It was the humans learned a wee bit of the noble art from O'Rigami, himself, to be sure—not the other way around. Indeed, isn't it named after him?"

"Well . . . " said Rolf slowly.

"And is it at all a human name it bears? When did you hear the likes of that from the Japanese islands? *O'Rigami*—why its ring is as pure Gremlin as that of the name of Lugh or Baneen."

"Ummm . . . "

"Tush and tush! Of course not," said Baneen. "Let's say no more on the subject. Indeed, it would be a proud human who'd dare to pretend to the beginnings of a skill like that of O'Rigami."

Baneen hooked a finger in the lowest buttonhole of Rolf's shirt and led him aside. The gremlin lowered his voice, almost whispering in Rolf's ear.

"A word to the wise—I'd watch your tongue, lad. There's nothing our Grand Engineer can't fold if he wishes. Rub him the wrong way and no telling what he'll do. How would you like Cape Kennedy folded into a flower pot? Or yourself into a postage stamp?"

Rolf's eyes widened. But before he could think of an answer, there was a shimmer in the air beside Baneen and the figure of a female gremlin with a pert, but sad, face and dressed in flowing green robes with a band of black around her left arm, took shape beside them.

"Ah, zair you are, Baneen," she said, in a soft, melancholy voice. "Sorrow and loneliness 'ave overwhelm me, waiteeng for you."

"Er—to be sure, to be sure," said Baneen. She tucked his right arm in hers and leaned against him. He looked uncomfortable. "But it's that terrible busy I've been, here, trying to work out a way to aid O'Rigami with the help of this lad, here—a human, you notice."

"I noteeced," said the female gremlin, now smiling sadly up at Rolf. "'Ow are you, 'uman? I 'ope you 'ave not lost too many loved ones to ze Terror?"

"His name's Rolf," said Baneen. "La Demoiselle here, lad, is a countess of fair Gremla. Naturally, the recent Revolution has awakened the deepest sympathies of her blue-green gremlin blood on behalf of those unfortunates of noble extraction—"

"Ah, deeply, deeply," sighed the Countess. "Seventeen times I 'ave cause ze blade of ze guillotine to stick wiz my gremleenish arts. In ozzer ways, also I 'ave also been useful. But 'ow little can any one person do? I am like ze Scarlet Pimpernel, zat noble Englishman—"

"Hear, hear," gruffed Shep behind them, obviously deeply moved.

"Ah, you too 'ave felt for these unfortunate ones, 'ave you, dog?" inquired La Demoiselle, turning to speak to Shep. Rolf took advantage of the opportunity to whisper puzzledly to Baneen.

"Is that the French Revolution she's talking about?" the boy asked. "I thought that all happened a couple of hundred years ago."

"It did," whispered back Baneen, producing a small green handkerchief and mopping his brow. "But the gremlinish feelings of such as the Countess, once awakened, do not go back to sleep easily. Let that be a lesson to you, lad—well, I must be going—"

"Ah, no you don't, naughtee one!" said La Demoiselle, turning back to snatch with both hands at Baneen as he faded out completely. "Oh! 'E 'as gone! Forgeeve me, M'sieu Rolf, but I mus' go find heem."

She vanished in her turn.

Rolf looked around him, but saw no one but Shep and O'Rigami nearby to explain matters to him.

"But what do you gremlins want me to do?" he asked O'Rigami.

"Ah, sooo," said O'Rigami, smiling widely. "Need some speciar suppries such as transistors. . . ." He pulled an almost invisibly small scrap of paper from a pocket in his white smock. But the paper grew strangely into a long strip as it touched Rolf's hand. A list of items was neatly hand-printed on it.

"Transistors and other necessary components," O'Rigami said. "If you wirr be so kind as to obtain them . . ."

"But wait a minute," said Rolf. "Why can't you get these things for yourselves?"

Baneen reappeared, alone, with a faint *pop*.

"Cold iron," said Baneen, simply. "Sure, and the places where the things are kept are full all round with iron this, and iron that. It would be like yourself having to fetch something you badly wanted out of the very center of a fiery furnace."

"All right, then," said Rolf, who had been thinking. "But why should I get them for you?"

"Indeed! Indeed!" exploded Shep. "The very idea, trying to put the boy to work for your blackguardly purposes! Naturally, he's not the sort to fetch and carry for a pack of gremlin scalawags! That's the spirit, lad. Tell them!"

"That's not what I meant," said Rolf. "What I meant—"

"Why now, you were only wondering what shape our gremlin gratitude would take, were you not?" cried Baneen. "To be sure, would we be accepting a favor and thinking of giving nothing in return? No, no, lad—what we have for you is no less than the Great Wish, itself. The same unlimited one wish given to any human clever enough to steal— ah, that is, return the Grand Corkscrew of Gremla, that symbol of kingship itself, should such as a human chance to find it after it had been lost. One wish—for whatever your heart desires!"

There was a sudden silent explosion in the background of Rolf's mind. All at once he had an image of his father and a lot of other people staring at him in awe after he had just announced that he would clean up all the pollution in the world with one snap of his fingers—and had just done it. But Shep was already growling back at the gremlin.

"What!" Shep was snorting. "He scorns your base attempt at bribery! Do you suppose a lad like this would think for a moment—"

"Just a minute, Shep," said Rolf hastily. "Baneen, could you make the world free of pollution—I mean, clean up all the pollution and make the environment safe forever, if I helped you?"

"The promise of a Baneen upon it, the moment our kite is safely headed for beautiful Gremla!"

"Do my ears deceive me?" demanded Shep. "Rolf, boy, think before you—"

"Indeed and indeed, the word of a Baneen, himself!" shot out Baneen quickly. "Ah, it's a bargain, then, and may the memory of it be warm in your heart for years to come. Now, off with you and gain the transistories, or whatever they're called, by tomorrow noon—"

"Just a second," said Rolf. "Where am I supposed to get them?"

"Is this," Shep was asking the sky, in a tragic voice, "the youngster I've stuck with through thick and thin? The boy I've raised like one of my own—"

"Now, Rolf me lad," said Baneen, briskly, "surely you know as well as anyone of a certain store not ten blocks from your very home, that has transistories and all such radio things and devices piled like coals in a coalshop, within its walls?"

"Oh," said Rolf. "Sure. But—wait another minute. These things may be expensive; and my bank account—"

"Rolf, Rolf," cried Baneen. "Did you think us the sort to ask for the use of the life savings of such a friend as yourself? Ah, never! Not a penny will any of these transistories cost your pocket. Just have yourself at the store this night about ten o'clock and we'll make it quite simple for you to slip inside and steal each and every one of them!"

4

Rolf looked nervously down the dark, deserted street. The whole town seemed to be asleep, and the only lights anywhere were the few street lamps glowing along the main avenue. One of the lamps was planted squarely in front of the hardware store.

"A black deed," muttered Mr. Sheperton. "Breaking into the hardware store to steal things for the gremlins. I thought I had brought you up better than that."

Rolf *shushed* him.

"You don't understand. Be quiet."

"Be quiet? I certainly will not be quiet!" Mr. Sheperton snapped back, but in a growly whisper. "Got half a mind to set up a howl that would bring on the police. If only the moon was full . . . "

Still standing uncertainly in the shadows of the Rocket City movie theater's lobby, Rolf felt his nerves jangling. Shep was right. Stealing was no way to go. But if a little theft now would make the future right and safe again for the brown pelican and all the rest of the world's creatures that were being threatened with destruction through pollution of one kind or another, certainly the end ought to justify the means?

"You were quiet enough at home tonight," he said to Shep. "Why didn't you say anything then?"

"Nothing for me to say," the dog replied. "Did you want *me* to cook dinner for you?"

Rolf's father had been out, as usual. The countdown for the Mars launch was too important for him to come home for dinner. His mother had been busy with the baby again, and when Rolf came home from Playalinda Beach he found that he had to fix his own dinner. He had opened a can of spaghetti and another of beef stew and eaten them both cold. Shep got his regular dogfood and half the beef stew.

Then Rolf had watched television for a while, fidgeting in the family room while his dinner made a cold lump inside him. He waited until it was late enough to slip out of the house. Rita Amaro had called to ask when his father would be on the TV news, and Rolf had hung up on her as quickly as he could.

Now, with everyone else asleep, Rolf still felt fidgety as he watched the empty street.

"If it's the police you're worried about," said Mr. Sheperton coldly, "I'm sure the gremlins will be keeping them busy on other things. They can cause all the mischief in the world whenever they choose to."

Rolf brightened a little. "Baneen said he'd help us. . . . "

"Us?" Mr. Sheperton's ears actually stood on end for an instant. "Not us, young man. You. You're the one who's decided on a life of crime."

"Aw, come on. It's only a few transistors."

"For a start."

Rolf didn't feel like arguing. He looked up and down the street once more. "Why'd they have to put that street lamp right in front of the hardware store?"

And just at the moment, that particular lamp suddenly dimmed, sputtered, and went completely dark. The hardware store's big front windows were swallowed by darkness.

"Baneen!" Rolf felt like shouting for joy. "He's helping us after all! Just like he said he would."

"Trust a gremlin to help you—to get into trouble," muttered Mr. Sheperton darkly.

But Rolf wasn't listening. He swiftly

crossed the street and, keeping to the shadows along the building walls as much as possible, he hurried down the street toward the hardware store. Shep padded along behind him, his claws making tiny clicking sounds on the pavement. There were no other sounds. The night was as quiet as it was dark.

They slipped into the entryway of the hardware store. It was set in between two big plate-glass display windows. It was wonderfully dark in there. So dark, in fact, that Rolf couldn't see the door very well at all. *How can I pick the lock if I can't see the keyhole?* he wondered.

"Have you thought about the store's burglar alarm?" asked Mr. Sheperton.

"Huh? Burglar alarm?" Rolf touched the door handle in the darkness. . . .

And the door swung open!

Rolf felt it move, swing inward, and almost lost his balance. He lurched forward, trying to avoid falling, and suddenly found himself inside the hardware store.

"It wasn't locked! They forgot to lock up!"

"More likely another sample of gremlin magic, I'd say," Mr. Sheperton grumbled. "They'll help you all they can . . . as long as you're doing what they want. What they're really doing, of course, is helping you to become as tricky and thieving as they are themselves."

"Aw, come on Shep. . . ."

The dog growled.

"Uh, Mr. Sheperton. All we have to do is find the right transistors and a little bit of wire. The store'll never miss what we take."

"But this is only the first step, Rolf. The gremlins won't let you stop at this. Once you've started working for them, once you've allowed them to bewitch you with their promises, you'll be hooked. They'll always promise more than they give, and they'll ask you to do bigger, riskier, more rascally tasks for them. In the end, they'll have everything they want, and you'll be behind bars. Or worse. I remember the case of one man, a young violinist . . ."

Rolf shook his head. "Never mind. I've got to find what we need."

He took the folded piece of paper from his shirt pocket and tried to read O'Rigami's careful printing. It was too dark to see much, but somehow the paper seemed to be much longer than it had been when he first took it.

"Better not show a light this close to the windows," Rolf said, more to himself than Mr. Sheperton.

So he made his way slowly down the store's main aisle, going by feel and memory more than sight. After a few bumps, he ducked behind the big counter where the cash register was. Squatting down on his heels, Rolf took his penlight from his pants pocket and clicked it on.

O'Rigami's list did indeed look a lot longer than he had remembered it. The green letters shimmered as the tiny light shone on them, and Rolf blinked in astonishment as three new items wrote themselves in at the bottom of the list.

Taking a big breath, like a man about to plunge off a high diving board, Rolf got to his feet and started hunting through the store's bins and drawers for the items O'Rigami needed.

It took a long time. Rolf had to work in the dark, risking the penlight only in quick flashes to read the labels on the storage bins and the boxes lined up on the shelves. And the gremlins' list seemed to grow longer every time he looked at it.

Slowly a tiny pile of transistors, connectors, wire, and other items—including a green felt-tip pen, of all things—grew on the top of the back counter, next to the cash register.

Rolf was putting two more transistors on the counter. They were as tiny as fleas. Mr. Sheperton growled, "Stand still!"

Rolf froze.

The dog seemed to be sniffing the air. Then he said, "Keep your light off and get behind the counter. Quickly!"

No sooner had Rolf ducked behind it than a beam of light swept across the store. Peeking around the side of the counter, Rolf could see that a police car had nosed up to the

curb and its headlights were shining right into the windows and door.

The door! Rolf felt his nerves jolting with electricity as he remembered that the door was unlocked. *What can I do? Maybe the back door . . .*

A policeman was already out of the car and heading for the door. Rolf didn't dare move; he couldn't even breathe. The officer walked slowly toward the unlocked door, glanced up at the still-dark street lamp, reached out and tried the door.

It stayed shut. He pushed on it, rattled it

a few times, then turned back toward the car.

"It's okay," Rolf heard his muffled calling to the other policeman in the car. "Locked up tight. Better call the utility company and tell 'em they've got a bum light here."

"Not now!" his partner yelled back. "The radio's going nuts. All the burglar alarms in the shopping center across town have gone off at once. We've gotta get there and find out what's going on."

The policeman jumped into the car. Before he could shut the door, his partner had put the car into reverse and backed away from the curb. They swung down the street with their red gumball light flashing.

Darkness returned to the hardware store. Slowly, Rolf stood up. His legs ached with nervous cramps. He was shivering and drenched with a cold sweat.

Mr. Sheperton got up too, and leaned his forepaws on the counter top. He huffed at the scattered pile of electronics components. "Quite a scare for a measly ten dollars worth of trinkets."

Rolf looked at the pile. Mr. Sheperton was right. All the junk on the table wouldn't cost much more than ten dollars.

He suddenly patted the dog's floppy-eared, furry head. "Come on Sh . . . Mr. Sheperton. Let's get out of here."

"And leave your booty?"

"We'll get it tomorrow morning. Legally. After the bank opens and I can raid my savings account. I didn't realize these things would be so cheap."

Sure enough, when Rolf tried the front door it was unlocked again. And as he and Mr. Sheperton trotted down the street toward home, the street lamp in front of the store turned on brightly.

Breakfast was about the only time that Rolf ever saw his father anymore. Tom Gunnarson had never been a loud, jovial man. But these days he was uptight, wound up, and hardly said a word to anyone as Mrs. Gunnarson put bowls of cereal on the table for her two men.

"How's the countdown going, Dad?" Rolf asked.

"Huh?" Tom Gunnarson seemed deep in private thought. He looked up at his son. "Oh, the countdown. Fine, right on schedule. Everything's working just right. No hitches at all. No gremlins anywhere."

Rolf nearly choked on a spoonful of cereal.

"G . . . gremlins?" he coughed.

"Mythical creatures," Mr. Gunnarson explained absently. "Whenever something goes wrong with a piece of machinery, the technicians say that gremlins have gotten into it. Gremlins get blamed for anything that goes wrong—they're supposed to be full of mischief. No such thing as gremlins, actually, of course."

Swallowing hard, Rolf stayed silent.

"No," his father went on, thoughtfully. "The countdown's been remarkably free of gremlins. Everything's going so smoothly that it's kind of spooky. Which reminds me—I may have a happy surprise for all of us, to announce to you in a day or two."

"If it's all going so smoothly, why can't you spend more time at home, then?" Rolf blurted.

"Rolf!" his mother snapped. "Don't be fresh. You know your father would be home if he could be. The launch . . . "

But Tom Gunnarson put a lean, strong hand on his wife's arm. "Actually, Rolf," he said, "it wasn't the launch itself that kept me busy last night." His voice sounded slightly blurred, tired. "We had a long session with the security people. . . . "

"Security?" Rolf squeaked. His heart gave a thump inside him.

"Yes. Somebody's been sneaking boatloads of tourists into the cleared area around Playalinda Beach. That's not really very dangerous right now, but the security people are getting very upset about it. That area has to be cleared before we can launch, and if some thieving boat captain is taking advantage of the tourists and holds up our launch . . . "
Rolf's father clenched his fist tightly enough

to bend metal. Fortunately he wasn't holding his spoon at that moment.

They finished breakfast in silence. Almost. The baby began crying as Rolf spooned the last of his milk-softened cereal flakes. Mrs. Gunnarson got up quickly and headed for the nursery. *Used to be my playroom,* Rolf couldn't help reminding himself.

His father got up a moment later. "See you later, son."

"Okay, Dad."

Tom Gunnarson called to his wife from the front door. She called back from the nursery, told him to try to get home early enough for a good night's rest. Then he was gone. Rolf sat in the kitchen. *Alone,* he thought, *again.* He pushed his chair back from the table and, without a word to his mother, went out the back door.

He was getting his bike out of the garage, when Rita came up. She was just Rolf's age—in fact, they had grown up together, but now she looked to him like a stranger.

"Hi," she said.

"Hi," he answered, busy rolling his bike out.

"Say, he was neat on television, last night," she said.

"Who?" he grunted, without looking at her.

"Your dad!" she looked surprised. "Didn't you watch him on TV last night? We saw him on the later news. And they had the same thing on again this morning, on the network show. Everybody in the country must have seen him this morning."

"Big deal," said Rolf.

"What d'you mean—big deal?" She stared at him.

"Big deal," he insisted. "You know what's important in the world today? Ecology, that's what. But you think you'd see anyone on the tube because he's doing work in ecology? But anybody connected with a space launch —that's neeaat." he drawled out the last word, sarcastically.

"Rolf, you—" She almost exploded. He looked at her, then. Rita Amaro was a happy girl, always smiling, her teeth flashing brightly against the dark tan of her skin. Rolf had decided secretly, last term in school after they had more or less gotten out of touch with each other, that she really was a pretty girl. When she grew up, she'd probably be beautiful enough to be a movie star or a stewardess, or something like that—and forget she had ever known anyone like him. Right now she looked ready to lose her temper. But she did not.

"He's your *father*, Rolf!" she said. "I'd think you'd be proud. Man, you're weird!"

"He doesn't know anything about ecology," muttered Rolf. "What's more, he doesn't care. He's just an engineer."

She opened her mouth and this time he did brace himself for an explosion, but instead, she closed her mouth again.

"Rolf," she said, almost gently. "You're . . . I don't know what—"

"Weird," Rolf got up on his bike and pushed off. "That's what I am. Weird. And my father's famous. Big deal!"

He left her standing in the driveway, looking after him as if she was still half-mad, half-something to which he could not put a name.

Shep appeared from somewhere as Rolf pedaled down the street toward the center of town, and raced alongside the bike. The morning sun wasn't too high yet; the day was still cool. A good breeze was blowing. Rolf wanted to get to the hardware store just as they were opening up. But he had to stop at the bank first.

There was a big cherrypicker crane standing in front of the hardware store, and the hard-hatted electrician up in the cab was yelling down to his assistant on the truck:

"I tell ya I can't find nothin' wrong with it! Whoever called in and said this lamp was out must've been kiddin'!"

"It was the cops called in," his helper yelled back.

The electrician shook his head. "Half the burglar alarms in town on the fritz and what're the fuzz doin'? Sendin' in phony complaints about street lamps!"

Rolf tried not to grin as he leaned his bike against the store front and walked in. Shep settled down on his belly beside the bike.

The pile of material was still on the back counter, beside the cash register. One of the young salesboys had just spotted it, and was standing there looking puzzled.

Rolf hurried back to him. "Uh, that's my stuff," he said. "I was in here yesterday just as they were closing up, and I didn't have enough money to buy all that stuff, so I asked the man to leave it there so I could pick it up this morning."

The salesboy frowned. He looked at the pile of electronic components, then at Rolf, then at the pile again.

"I was here last night, and I helped clean up after we closed shop. I don't remember . . ." Then, with a shrug, he said, "Well, whatever. I'll ring it up for you."

It came to exactly $13.13, which didn't leave much in Rolf's savings account.

Shaking his head unhappily at the thought of how long it had taken him to save that money, Rolf stashed the paper bag on his bike's rattrap and pushed on for Playalinda Beach.

"Come on, Shep," he called. "I want to see what they're going to do with this stuff."

5

As he pedaled out toward the Playalinda Beach area and the Gremlin Hollow, Rolf heard Shep mumbling under his breath while the dog trotted alongside the bike.

"What's the matter now?" Rolf asked.

"Your manners," answered Mr. Sheperton. "An absolute disgrace. The way you treated that girl . . . "

"Who? Rita?"

"You know very well that I mean Rita. You were shockingly rude to her."

Rolf felt a twinge of guilt, but he said nothing. With a shake of his head, he said, "Ahh . . . who cares?"

"You should," Mr. Sheperton replied. "And

you do, I know. You can't hide your feelings from me, Rolf. You like her very much. She's the one you were showing off for when you took that fall off the high board—"

Rolf's bad leg ached suddenly at the memory of it. "I wasn't showing off!" he growled. But both he and the dog knew he didn't mean it.

Mr. Sheperton kept grumbling as Rolf pedaled along the highway.

"Uh, Shep—I mean, Mr. Sheperton," Rolf said after a few minutes of hard pumping up a small rise in the road. "Don't say anything to the gremlins about me and Rita, will you? They don't have to know that she was even around when I hurt my leg."

Shep snorted. "It's a bit late to keep the matter secret, with that trickster Baneen riding around on your handlebars all this time."

"Baneen? Handlebars?" Rolf blinked.

Something like a small noiseless explosion popped in front of him and Baneen was suddenly smiling up at him. Just as Shep had said, the gremlin was perched on the right handlebar of Rolf's bike.

"Well, well, well, well!" cried Baneen cheerfully. "And a beautiful day it is, to be sure. Ah now, and why would you be wanting to keep the fact of your friendship with such a fine young lady, a secret, lad?"

"Never mind," snapped Rolf, recovering from his surprise. "What about you? Where did you come from? And how come you're here, anyway?"

"Why it's pure chance, pure chance—and just a mite of worry mixed in," said Baneen. "We gremlins having the second sight and all, it was a bit of a blow to me when I chanced to look in on you this morning and found you hadn't got the wee things we asked you to pick up for us. Ah, what will we do now, poor, helpless gremlins that we are—I asked myself? Lugh must hear of this, I said; and I went to find him. But before I did indeed find him, I changed my mind. It's a terrible thing, the wrath of mighty Lugh—"

"Poor, helpless gremlin that he is, of course," sneered Shep.

"Ah, don't be twisting my words now, don't," said Baneen. "I thought of the wrath of Lugh and I thought of the lad, here, and I thought it would do no harm to speak to Rolf first. So I made a small spell in a twinkling to bring me to you—and here now, I find you have the little things after all."

"That's right," said Rolf. "They're on the back of my bike, there."

"So indeed I see," said Baneen, casting a bright inquisitive glance past Rolf's elbow to the brown paper bag pinned in the bike's rattrap. He switched his gaze to the scrub grass and bushes beside the road. "You can turn off here, lad."

"Here?" Rolf asked, surprised. He looked

and saw a trail he didn't recognize snaking away through the brush.

"It's a bit of a shortcut we've fixed up to our Hollow," said Baneen.

Rolf turned down the trail, which turned and twisted in strange ways. In seconds, it seemed, he was completely out of sight of the road they had just left.

"How far—" he started to ask.

"Not far, not far at all!" said the gremlin. "In just a second now, we'll be there. Once again it's yourself who'll be setting eyes on the high mysteries and secret workings of us gremlin-folk, that none but you know about. And it's certain sure that I am that none but you does know; because a fine lad such as yourself wouldn't have told anybody about us, would you now?" His voice and eyes suddenly seemed sharpened all together. "Not even that fine young lady you were talking with less than an hour ago?"

"Rita? Why would I—" Rolf broke off suddenly, stopping his bike and putting his feet down on the sandy soil. For they had come suddenly upon the lip of the Gremlin Hollow. Down below, he could see hordes of gremlins hard at work stretching out the large kite-shape of O'Rigami's. The Grand Engineer stood patiently off to one side, watching the work. Further away, Lugh was busily directing still more gremlins who carried, dragged, and tugged strangely shaped chests and boxes across the sand. A few gremlins were floating a foot or so off the ground, guiding green-colored crates that floated alongside them.

Everything in the Hollow was noise and bustle, a thousand tiny voices chattering and screeching at once. And, as usual, the gremlin magic was playing tricks with Rolf's vision. The kite once again looked as big as a jetliner, while the Hollow itself seemed no more than thirty or forty feet across.

Rolf started to pick up the sentence where he had left it, but before he could get out another word, Shep set up a furious barking.

"What's that? Stop! Stop immediately, do you hear me! Turn that thing round and get it out of here. . . ."

Rolf and Baneen turned together to look, because Shep was facing away from the Hollow, in the direction of the beach.

"Great Gremla protect us!" yelped Baneen. "It's a monster, headed right this way to destroy us all!"

"It's a bulldozer," Rolf yelled.

The machine was indeed roaring in their direction. It topped the rise that separated the Hollow from sight of the beach, and bore straight down toward the Hollow itself.

"Hey, it's going to tear up the kite!" Rolf cried.

"Stop! Stop, I say!" barked Mr. Sheperton. But the bulldozer came right on.

"It's no good! It's no good!" cried Baneen, hopping madly on Rolf's handlebars. "Sure and we're all invisible here within the magic wards about this place. We're going to be scooped up like peas on a spade and drowned in the sand!"

6

The bulldozer roared and clattered like an angry demon with a hide of yellow steel. Instead of breathing fire, though, it puffed dirty black smoke into the clear sky.

It bore straight down on the Gremlin Hollow, pushing a huge pile of sand ahead of it on its wide ugly blade. Gremlins were dashing everywhere, screaming in terror and rage. O'Rigami was madly trying to fold up his kite before the 'dozer's treads ground it to shreds. Baneen huffed and puffed and made wild motions with his magical hands. The bulldozer didn't even slow down, although the driver sneezed once.

Rolf saw the great machine boring straight

at him, like a moving mountain of sand threatening to bury him.

Mr. Sheperton barked furiously. Baneen fluttered up into the air, screeching, "It's no good, no good at all! He can't see us or hear us!"

And then Lugh's giant voice roared out, "WHAT IN THE NAME OF THE DUSTY SKIES OF GREMLA IS GOING ON HERE?"

Before anyone could utter another word, Lugh looked up at the approaching bulldozer. His brows pulled down into a terrible scowl. His cheeks puffed out and his nostrils flared dangerously.

"A great ugly mechanical monster, is it? Well, we'll just see about that."

The bulldozer had just reached the edge of the Hollow, still pushing sand ahead of it. Some of the sand was already spilling into the Hollow and pouring over some of the gremlins who were shrieking and scattering every which way. O'Rigami's hands were flying faster than the eye could follow, folding up the precious kite. Rolf stood straddling his bike, with Baneen floating up at about his eye level and Mr. Sheperton growling and tense beside him.

Lugh thrust out his jaw and eyed the machine angrily. Fists planted dangerously on his hips, he strode off to one side of the oncoming monster, fury and vengeance in every stiff-legged, four-inch-long step.

"What's he going to do?" Rolf wondered.

"Not . . ." Baneen started, then pressed both his fists into his mouth and stared at Lugh, goggle-eyed. He zipped downward and touched his feet to the sandy ground.

Lugh thrust out his right arm and pointed at the yellow bulldozer. His voice became mighty and terrible:

"MAY THE GREAT AND THUNDEROUS CURSE OF GREMLA FALL UPON YOUR HEAD!"

Baneen fainted.

Mr. Sheperton snorted, almost like a sneeze.

Rolf hiccupped.

And the bulldozer slowed. Its roar became a rumble, then a squeak. The smoke-belching exhaust stack seemed to tremble, then shot a sheet of blue flame fifty feet into the sky. Both treads of the bulldozer snapped, and all the wheels fell off.

The driver yelled something wild and leaped from his seat as if his pants were on fire. He dived headfirst into the sand. The bulldozer's engine dissolved in a huge cloud of smoke. The metal sides of the machine fell away and turned to rust as they hit the ground. The whole machine seemed to crumble, like a balloon when the air goes out of it.

In less than a minute there was nothing

left except a badly frightened driver and a mess of steaming, rusting machinery that was fast disappearing into the sand.

Lugh nodded his head once, the way a man does when he knows he's finished a task and done it well.

"Be that a lesson to all of you," he said firmly, "gremlin, man and beast alike. Lugh of the Long Hand is not to be pushed about."

Rolf simply stared. The bulldozer was completely gone now, hardly even a wisp of steam left to mark where it once stood. The driver was sitting on the sand, looking as if he didn't believe any of this, even though he had seen it. He was a young man, Rolf saw, with long black hair and a sun-bronzed skin. He kept shaking his head and staring at the spot where the bulldozer had been.

While Rolf watched, Baneen stirred himself and climbed weakly to his feet, using Rolf's leg for support. "I was afraid Lugh would invoke the Great Curse. It's a wonder it didn't bury us all with its terrible magic."

Another man was running up to the bulldozer driver. He was older, black skin shining with perspiration where his shirt was open and showing his chest.

"Hey, Charlie, what did you stop for? Where's the 'dozer?" Charlie extended a shaking arm and pointed. "It . . . it was right there. . . ." His voice was trembling.

"Was?" The black man took a quick look

around. "Where is it now?"

"Gone. Dissolved. Fell apart and rusted away—just like that." Charlie tried to snap his fingers, but it didn't work.

The black man stooped down and picked up a tiny fragment of rusted yellow-painted metal. "Rusted out?" His voice had suddenly gone high-pitched with shock. "A whole 'dozer don't rust out, not all at once."

"Thi-this one did!"

Charlie stared at his partner, then reached down and yanked him up onto his feet. "Come on, friend. You been out in the sun too long. We better get out of here before the ranger patrol flies past."

As the two men disappeared back over the rise, Lugh bellowed to the other gremlins, "Well, what are you standing there for, with your mouths hanging open? Back to work, all of you, before I turn you into toadstools."

Gremlins seemed to sprout out of the sand everywhere and hustled about busily. O'Rigami began to unfold his kite once more, just as calmly as if nothing had ever disturbed him.

"Lugh, me princely protector," Baneen called out, "You wouldn't be wanting that great heap of sand to stay there, would you now?"

"Well said. Get rid of it, trickster. And the beast's tracks, too."

Baneen smiled happily and danced a small

circle around himself. "Ah yes, we wouldn't want them that near us, again, would we? Even to cover their own tracks."

Rolf looked up and saw the pile of sand growing dim and shimmering in the heat from the blazing sun. Before he could blink three times, the little mountain had completely disappeared. And so had the tracks of the bulldozer's caterpillar treads.

"Won't they wonder how their tracks vanished?" Rolf asked.

"Ah, no, lad," Baneen answered lightly. "Men never question their good luck. It's only the bad luck they wonder about."

"Maybe you ought to leave the tracks, though," said Rolf. "So I've got something to show to the authorities when I report this."

"Report? Report, lad? Sure, and there's nothing to report," said Baneen, hastily. "Their murderous machine's nothing but a pile of rust now, and the villains themselves have gone. Or, indeed, maybe they were no villains at all, but a couple of humans from the ranger station down the beach a ways, just doing their jobs."

Mr. Sheperton growled, swinging his head about so that he and Baneen stood nose to nose, almost touching.

"Why were they so anxious to get away before the next patrol plane came over, then, might I ask?"

"That's right," said Rolf.

"Hmm, they did say something like that, didn't they?" Baneen cocked his head to one side, as if thinking. "Scalawags! To think they'd push sand into our Hollow, our one little wee spot on the whole face of this vast and watery . . . But come, come, there's wisdom in letting well enough alone. They're gone now."

"But you can't let them get away with doing something like that, here in the very heart of the Wildlife Preserve," said Rolf. "I've just got to report them. What if they come back?"

"Ah, now, they won't be back at all, at all," said Baneen.

"How do you know?" Rolf demanded.

"Well, it's my gremlinish second sight tells me. Indeed—" Baneen closed his eyes and touched his nose thoughtfully with the tip of one green finger. "I see the Hollow here . . . and the beach . . . tomorrow . . . and the next day. . . . " He opened his eyes. "No sign of the rascals or another such fearful mechanical monster. You can rest easy, lad, and not trouble yourself further."

"Why," demanded Rolf, "are you so set against me reporting them?"

"Yes," rumbled Mr. Sheperton. "Answer that, will you? You're not telling everything you know. No more gremlin trickery, Baneen. Who are these men, and what are they up to?"

"And what makes you think I'd know?" Baneen said.

"I *know* you know," the dog answered.

"Do you now?"

"Yes I do."

"Hmp! These English and their superior airs."

Mr. Sheperton growled, low and menacing. Baneen danced away from him and skipped behind Rolf.

"Well now . . . I'm not saying that there's anything I know for certain. But—well, sure and it'll do no harm to show you something."

Baneen trotted out toward the far edge of the Hollow, and Rolf followed him up the slope, across a couple of sandy little hillocks, and out toward the beach.

Padding along beside Rolf, Mr. Sheperton grumbled "That little green rascal knows far more than he's told us."

"But," Rolf said, squinting against the glare of the dazzling sun that beat off the white sand, "If he really knew what was going on, would he have let the bulldozer get so close to nearly burying the Hollow?"

Mr. Sheperton seemed to shake his head. "There's no telling what a gremlin will do— except that it will be bad for any humans nearby."

Rolf turned to stare at Baneen, just ahead. The boy could hear the hissing boom of the surf now, and felt the tangy salt breeze on his face. He started to run up toward where Baneen was, but the gremlin turned and put a finger to his lips, waving at Rolf to get down.

Bursting with curiosity, Rolf crawled on his stomach up to the top of the dune. Laid flat out, he peered through the grass. Mr. Sheperton lay beside him, panting wetly in his ear.

At first glance, the beach looked perfectly ordinary. But then Rolf saw that someone had dug a narrow channel into the beach, and put a sort of bridge over it. The bridge was covered with a thin layer of sand. The surf was breaking far out in the water, at least a hundred yards before the channel.

"Somebody's built a breakwater out there, like an underwater sandbar," Rolf said.

"Yes," agreed Mr. Sheperton. "And a place to bring in a boat and hide it under that sand bridge."

"Camouflage."

The putt-putting of an engine made Rolf turn his head toward the right. A boat was puffing through the sea, heading straight for the disguised channel. As the three of them watched, the boat came in and two grimy looking sailors in tattered shirts and shorts leaped from its deck and tied it securely to the posts that held up the bridge.

"They're the villains that sent the mechanical beast at us," Mr. Sheperton muttered.

"They wanted more sand to cover their bridge and dump into their breakwater."

Another man appeared on the ship's deck. He was chunky and fat-faced. He wore a blue jacket and white slacks, and even had a perky little captain's hat perched on his head. He squealed orders at the two sailors, who were now back on the boat, sweating and struggling with heavy boxes.

"Come on, come on," the captain piped at them in a nasty nasal, high-pitched voice. "I want all the telescopes and binoculars stored away here so we can use all our space to carry people on the day of the launch. Move it, move it!"

"So that's it," Mr. Sheperton said. "He's the one that your father was worrying about. Bringing in tourists to watch the launch from here on the beach."

"There must be more to it than that, though," said Rolf. "They wouldn't go to that much trouble for a boatload of tourists two or three times a year."

"Quite right! How about that, you gremlin?" Mr. Sheperton demanded of Baneen.

"Ah well," said Baneen uncomfortably, "sure and the one in the sailor hat there does bring in people with guns to hunt and fish, now and then."

Rolf felt suddenly sick—in his mind's eye he saw images of the brown pelican and the young piglets, bloody and slaughtered.

"But this is a Preserve!" he said, fiercely. "It's the one little piece of the environment around here that's unprotected! And you say I shouldn't report someone like that?"

"But we've never let them harm the wee beasts and birds," said Baneen, hastily. "Not since we've been here has one of his hunters gained a single prey—"

"That doesn't make any difference!" said Rolf. "I don't care what you've been doing. I'm reporting this man and his crew."

"No lad, you can't!" said Baneen. "Listen to me, now. We mustn't have police and rangers and suchlike stamping up and down the beach here and tramping all over our Hollow."

"I'm sorry," said Rolf. "But this is one thing I just have to do."

"But you'll listen to me for a moment before doing it, won't you?" pleaded Baneen. "Wait, Rolf, just a second whilst I bring you one who can plead our desperate case better than myself. . . ."

"Don't listen to him, boy," growled Mr. Sheperton.

"I don't see how they've managed to avoid being seen, anyway, before this," said Rolf. "You ought to be able to see that oil slick and boat smoke from a ranger plane pretty easily."

He turned to look suspiciously at Baneen.

"Now, now!" cried the gremlin. "It was just the slightest touch of magic we've used in their favor, to be sure—just enough to keep them from being seen. Nothing invisible, mind you. Just a wee distraction or two to make the patrol rangers look the other way as they fly past the noise and dirt. But just a minute. Wait right here—"

He disappeared with a popping noise.

"Let's not wait for him, Shep—Mr. Sheperton, I mean," said Rolf.

"Quite right!" rumbled Mr. Sheperton. "Enough of the blackguard's lies and evasions—"

Baneen popped back into existence, pulling along with him another gremlin—also wearing green, it was true, but with a long, sad, greenish blue cloak around his shoulders, long dark hair hanging down under his hat, and a violin case under his arm.

"Rolf, let me—" puffed Baneen, breathlessly, "introduce that grand—gremlin musician—O'Kkane Baro."

The other gremlin took his hat off his head and swept it before him as he bowed gracefully. He had a handsome, if tragic, face.

"Glorious to acquaint you!" he cried, in a rich, full voice, "Glorious! If my heart was not breaking, I would dance with joy. But who dances in a world like this? I ask you!"

He sat down mournfully in the sand, laying the violin case aside. Rolf stared at him.

"Hist!" whispered Mr. Sheperton in his

ear. "Don't let this rascal fool you, either. He's a gypsy gremlin. Do you know what Hokkane Baro means, in the Romany tongue?"

"Ah, but the heart of our poor friend is indeed breaking," said Baneen sorrowfully. "All these thousands of years that he has lived, now, only in the hope of seeing Gremla again—"

"Ah, Gremla, my sunshine, my beautiful!" exclaimed O'Kkane Baro resonantly, covering his eyes with one hand. "Never to see you again. Never . . . never!"

"Hokkane Baro means," whispered Mr. Sheperton severely, "the *big trick*, a con game they used to play on gullible peasants."

Rolf nodded. He had no doubt that Mr. Sheperton was right. But O'Kkane Baro's unhappiness was so convincing he began to feel a twinge of guilt in spite of himself.

"You'll see it," he said to the dark-haired gremlin. "Don't worry."

"Ah, but will he?" said Baneen. "Now that you're determined and all to report what you've seen. Sure, and it's only a matter of minutes after the authorities come prowling around here that our magic will be spoiled and our last chance at Gremla lost for good."

"Ah . . ." said O'Kkane Baro, unshielding his eyes. "But, why should we weep?" he spread his arms. "Let us laugh . . . ha, ha!" Rolf thought he had never heard such mournful laughter in his life.

"Yes, laugh!" cried O'Kkane Baro, rising to his feet. "Laugh, dance, be gay—sing! Music!"

He clapped his hands; at the sound, the lid of his violin case opened and a gremlin-sized violin floated out and up into the air. A gremlin-sized bow floated after it and poised itself over the strings.

"Play, gypsy!" commanded O'Kkane Baro, stamping his foot on the sand. The violin began to play, a wild, thrilling air. "Weep, gypsy—" The violin switched suddenly to wailing chords. Tears began to run down O'Kkane Baro's cheeks.

"Gremla . . . lovely Gremla . . . nevermore shall we set eyes upon thee . . . " he sobbed.

The music was overwhelming. Baneen was also crying. Tears were running as well out of Mr. Sheperton's nose and Rolf was blinking desperately to keep from joining them in tears.

"Wait . . . " begged Rolf. "Wait. . . . "

"Why wait?" keened Baneen. "All is over. And just because someone could not go two days before reporting some scoundrels. Ah, the whole gremlin race, robbed of its last, last chance! Didn't I say we'd see none of the animals or birds would come to harm? But did that soften the hard heart of someone I need not name? No—"

"Wait!" gulped Rolf. "All right. Two days.

I can wait two days—but stop that violin!"

"Ah yes, stop the instrument, O'Kkane Baro!" sobbed Baneen. "It's myself can barely stand the sorrow of it, either."

Weeping, O'Kkane Baro waved at the violin, which stopped playing and packed itself, with its bow, back into its case. In the silence, a high-pitched voice, the voice of the boat captain came clearly to their ears.

" . . . there! Right over the ridge there. Don't just stand there, get over after them! You heard the music coming from there until just a second ago!"

Rolf leaped to his feet and stared over the crest of the dune. The two sailors they had seen, the boat captain right behind them, were coming toward the dune. They all shouted when they saw Rolf.

"They spotted me!" Rolf cried. "What'll we do now?"

"Try an old gremlin trick, lad." advised the voice of Baneen behind him. *"Run!"*

7

Rolf took a fast look at the two burly sailors climbing the dune toward him. He started running down the other side of the dune, but the loose sand slowed him down.

He glanced over his shoulder and saw that the sailors had topped the rise and weren't far behind him. And they were gaining fast.

Baneen was dithering around, running in excited circles, waving his hands helplessly.

And Mr. Sheperton?

Rolf heard the dog barking furiously, the way he barked at automobiles that went down their home street too fast. Turning slightly, Rolf saw Mr. Sheperton charging at the two sailors, his bared teeth looking ferocious, even in his fuzzy mop of a head.

The sailors backed off for a moment. Mr. Sheperton surprised them, maybe even scared them. Then one of them pulled something long and menacing from his belt. Rolf couldn't tell whether it was a knife or a club.

"Shep . . . no!"

But Mr. Sheperton wasn't backing away. As long as Rolf was in danger, and he himself was conscious, the dog would attack the sailors.

"Baneen . . . do something!"

Suddenly Mr. Sheperton's open mouth started to spout foam. His barking began to sound more like gargling.

The sailor with the club, or whatever it was, went round-eyed.

"Mad dog!" he yelled. Spinning around, he raced back toward the safety of the boat. His friend went with him.

Mr. Sheperton raced after them, nipping at their heels, until they got to the top of the dune. Then he stood his ground and barked at them several more times. Rolf knew what Mr. Sheperton was saying:

"And don't come back! Blackguards! Cowards!"

Satisfied that everything was in proper shape, Mr. Sheperton trotted back down the sandy hill to Rolf and Baneen. Only then did Rolf realize that if the dog was really foaming at the mouth, it meant he was seriously ill.

"Shep . . . are you . . . ?"

"I don't know how many times it will be necessary to tell you," the dog said, a bit cross and out of wind, "that my name is Mr. Sheperton. And you, Baneen, if you don't mind, would you kindly remove this ridiculous shaving lather you've put on my face? Tastes of lime. Ugh."

"Ah, for such a grand hero as yourself, Mr. Sheperton, it was hardly necessary for me to do anything at all." Baneen wiggled his fingers and the foam instantly dried into crystal flakes that were carried away by the wind.

And suddenly Rolf dropped to his knees and hugged the shaggy old dog. "Shep, Shep . . . I thought you were sick."

For once, Mr. Sheperton didn't correct the boy. He sat there and let Rolf hold him. His tail even wagged once or twice. Sounding rather embarrassed, he said at last, "Well, harumph . . . I suppose we'd better get away from here before those rascals work up the nerve to come back."

On the way back to the Hollow, Baneen kept talking about O'Rigami's space kite and how wonderful it would be to return to Gremla.

"And the most wonderful part of it all," the gremlin said, dancing lightly over the sand, "is that yourself will be in complete charge of the entire launching of the great, powerful rocket. The most important man of all, that'll be you, Rolf me bucko. Er . . . once you've attached the kite to the rocket properly, of course."

Rolf nodded. But inwardly he was wondering how he could possibly get to his father's rocket and attach the kite, even if O'Rigami made it invisible. Gremlin magic wasn't going to be enough for *that* job.

Mr. Sheperton stayed strangely quiet as they approached the Hollow. Rolf could see gremlins scurrying about, busy with a thousand unguessable tasks. Lugh stood in the middle, as usual, in a small mound of sand, pointing here, shouting there, his tiny bulldog's face red with scowling, his chin whiskers bristling.

Rolf picked up his bike and said farewell to Baneen. The gremlin, jigging happily, reminded him:

"Don't be forgetting tomorrow, now. Tomorrow O'Rigami will have the grand kite finished, and tomorrow night you'll be helping us to attach it properly to the rocket. Ah, Gremla, land of' me youth! Soon we'll be back enjoying your dusty delights."

"Sure," Rolf said as he got on the bike. "Tomorrow."

He pedaled up and away from the Gremlin Hollow and got back on the road that led to the highway. But when he thought of the men with the boat and his own promise not to report them, he was conscious of an ugly, hollow feeling inside him.

Rolf's father wasn't home for dinner again that night. After helping his mother clean up the kitchen, Rolf went outside for a walk. The sun was low in the southwest, the breeze already had a bite of evening's coolness.

Mr. Sheperton came padding up to him, but Rolf said. "No, Shep. Stay. I want to think, not argue."

The dog muttered something about calling people by their proper names, as he trotted stiffly back toward the house.

Rolf walked out on the narrow sidewalk that fronted the lawn, and headed down the street slowly. "How deep am I getting myself into this?" he whispered to himself. It all seems so crazy. For one thing, suppose something goes wrong when I'm helping the gremlins and I get caught?"

There was only one tree in this part of town worth climbing, a sturdy old live oak that had been growing for maybe fifty years before the houses had been built and the streets put in. Miraculously, it had escaped the bulldozers and builder, probably because it looked too big and tough to knock over easily.

The tree happened to be right next to the Amaros' old two-story house, close to Rita's window. Rolf hesitated in the dark at the foot of the tree, remembering all the times he had climbed up there for secret talks with her, back when they both had been real young kids. But now he needed to talk to her again, and the tree looked as climbable as ever.

He climbed up easily, but found that he'd gotten too big to crawl out on the limb that practically brushed her window. And the window was closed, because the house had recently been air conditioned.

Can't use our old signal, Rolf knew, remembering the way he'd whistle like a bobolink. *How can I call her?*

While he sat there hunched up on the big branch near the tree trunk, Rita opened the window. Over her shoulder she called, "Okay, Momma. I've got my window open. Tell me when the air conditioner is working again, and I'll shut it."

Rolf thought he could hear Baneen giggling in the shadows of the tree.

"Hey, Rita!" he whispered.

She jerked back a little in surprise. "Rolf? What are you doing there?"

"I wanted to talk with you."

She smiled, and it looked better than moonlight to Rolf. "Just the way we used to," she said. "Wait a minute."

She ducked inside for a moment, then crawled out on the window ledge.

"Hey, no . . . the branch can't hold . . ."

But Rita already had one bluejeaned leg on the branch. "I'm not as heavy as you are."

Or as careful, Rolf thought. But she crawled out on the branch. It dipped and swayed under her weight, but Rita calmly shinnied up until she was sitting safely next to Rolf.

"We haven't done this in ages," she said happily.

"Yeah," Rolf nodded. It *was* fun. Almost, it took him back two years, to before he had started going out to the Preserve, alone.

More seriously, Rita said, "I was beginning to think you didn't like me anymore. You've stayed away so much lately. . . . I'm sorry I said you were weird."

Rolf had forgotten that. "Oh, that's okay."

"You really have been acting strange. You know?"

"I guess so. . . . " He didn't know where to begin, how to tell her.

For a moment they just sat there, bare feet dangling in the cool evening air.

"Rita?" Rolf said. "Listen. There is uh . . . something I need your help for."

"Sure Rolf. What is it?"

"Your father's still on the night shift, isn't he?"

"Yes." Then she added proudly, "He's been promoted to sergeant. He's got a whole shift of guards under him now."

"But he's still working right at the launch

pad, isn't he?"

"Yes."

Hesitating for a moment more, Rolf finally decided to take the plunge. "Look . . . I need to get up close to the rocket. Up onto the top platform of the checkout tower. Tomorrow night."

"Tomorrow night?" Rita's voice sounded shocked. In the darkness it was difficult to make out the expression on her face. "But that's the night before the launch! Nobody's allowed . . . "

Slowly, and as carefully as he could, Rolf explained to Rita about the gremlins and how they wanted to use the Mars rocket to help the return to Gremla.

He was earnestly explaining about O'Rigami and the space kite when Rita began laughing. He stared at her, and she laughed so hard he had to put out a hand to keep her from falling off the branch. Her shoulders were pumping up and down, and she put a hand over her mouth to keep from making so much noise that her parents would catch them. "Mmpff, mmppfff," came the sound from behind her hand.

"Hey, it's not funny," Rolf said.

"Oh, Rolf," she gasped. "When you want to put somebody on, you sure can do it. . . . " She started giggling again.

"'Tis no joke, me lovely maid." It was Baneen's voice, coming from right behind

Rolf's ear.

Rolf turned his head slightly and saw that the gremlin was perched on his shoulder. Strangely, he felt no weight on the shoulder at all. Then, looking back at Rita, he could see that her eyes had gone white and round. Her laughter was stopped. Her mouth was open, and her eyes were enormous.

"Allow me the grand pleasure of being introduced to this charming young lady," Baneen said.

Still holding Rita by one arm, Rolf said, "This is Baneen—one of the gremlins. Baneen, this is Rita Amaro."

"Charmed, I'm certain," said Baneen, and he took his little green cap off, making a low sweeping bow to the girl.

Rita recovered her voice. "You . . . you're real!"

"As real as your beautiful brown eyes, Rita me girl. And as happy as your darling laughter. But all the gremlins on this vast dreary world would be sadder than a mud toad's croak if it weren't for this fine, brave lad here."

"Aw, come on, Baneen," Rolf said.

"You . . . you really want Rolf to attach this . . . kite thing . . . to the Mars rocket?"

"Exactly!" Baneen smiled at her. "What a clever lass she is! Sure, and you've caught on right away, my dear."

"I'll be in charge of the final countdown,"

Rolf said. "I'll have to delay the launch six minutes from its scheduled liftoff time. Right, Baneen?"

"That's what O'Rigami figures—although frankly I've no head for numbers and I can't be sure if six minutes is the right amount. But what difference, six minutes or sixty? The rocket won't go until *you* give the word, Rolf, me bucko."

Rita seemed aghast. "Rolf, you could foul up the whole launching!"

"Ah, no," Baneen assured her. "Just a wee delay and a slight detour. No problem at all."

She shook her head. "This could be really serious."

"I'm going to do it," Rolf said quietly. It was on the tip of his tongue to tell her about the Great Wish the gremlins had promised him. Then he remembered that she had always admired his father—who obviously had no concern for ecology.

"There's nothing to it, I tell you," Baneen repeated. "Why, with gremlin magic at work, we could put everyone in the launch center to sleep for a fortnight—ah, but we don't want to do that, desperate though we are."

"They've got to get off our planet and back to Gremla," said Rolf. "And I'm going to help them."

"I don't understand why. . . . "

"Well, lass, you see now, it's Lugh—big, blustering oaf that he is. A terrible-tempered gremlin. Terrible temper." Baneen shuddered. "He's a gremlin prince, you know. But our king, Hamrod the Heartless, was always playing tricks on Lugh. Loved to see the great burly Lugh of the Long Hand turn red with frustration and anger. So it was that Lugh stole the Great Corkscrew of Gremla, took himself and his entire household—all of us—and in one great magic huff-and-puff brought us all to Earth, these thousands of years ago."

Rolf and Rita listened, fascinated.

"Well, once safely here on this awful watery planet, Lugh found out two things. One, there were plenty of oafish humans about, to serve as the butt of *his* jokes. No longer was Lugh at the mercy of Hamrod; now he had humans at his mercy. The tables were turned, so to speak.

"But the second thing he found out that here on this watery place, gremlin magic is pitifully weak—water ruins magic, don't you know—so our tricks amount to mere pranks. Watered down, they are."

"Like wiping out a bulldozer?" Rolf asked.

"Aye, the Great Curse. Pitiful, wasn't it? Why, on safe, dusty Gremla when the Great Curse is invoked, forty comets explode and the stars dance for a month. But here . . ." Baneen's voice dropped to a melancholy whisper, "well, about all we can do is play little pranks. Stopping clocks and making machines behave poorly, suchlike. Not even Lugh's great magic can get all of us at once more than ten feet off the ground. That's why we need your mighty rocket to help us get back to Gremla."

Rita asked, "But why does Lugh want to return to Gremla if your king is so nasty to him?"

"Ah, there's the nub of it all," Baneen said, dabbing at the corner of one eye with his eyebrow. "A clever girl you are, Miss

Rita. You see, underneath all of Lugh's bad temper and bluster, beats a heart of fairy gold. He knows how miserable all we gremlins have been here on dripping old Earth, and he's willing to sacrifice himself to save all of us. I doubt that we could last another few hundred years here on Earth, with all this water about. Doubt it strongly, that I do."

"I don't know . . ." Rita said uncertainly.

"Ah, but I do know what Lugh will do if he can't get human help for our return to Gremla," Baneen said, with a shudder in his voice. "It'll be terrible. He'll use every grain of gremlin magic to make life as miserable as possible for you humans. Many's the time I've heard him mutter," and Baneen's voice took on some of the deep roughness of Lugh's, "If we can't use that rocket to get us back to Gremla, the humans will never get to use it to take themselves to Mars."

It was Rolf's turn to be shocked. "You never told me that! You mean if we don't help you . . ."

"Lugh will keep the rocket from flying off," Baneen finished for him. "And it's himself has got the power to do it. That great rocket will just sit there and grow moss on it before Lugh lets it go."

8

"I wish you'd stay close to home today," Mrs. Gunnarson said to Rolf as he ate breakfast. His father hadn't come home at all. He was staying at the Space Center for the final thirty-six hours of countdown.

"Aw, Mom," Rolf said, between spoonfuls of cereal, "There's nothing to do around here. All the other guys'll bug me about Dad being on TV and being Launch Director. . . ."

His mother looked at him penetratingly.

"Is that what they do?" she asked. " 'Bug' you?"

Rolf stared down at the cereal.

"You don't know what it's like, when your father's . . . " he muttered, letting the sentence trail off.

"You really should learn to get along with the other boys," she said. "For that matter, you should learn to get along better with your father."

"He doesn't need me," mumbled Rolf under his breath to the cereal.

"What?"

"Nothing." Rolf pushed away from the kitchen table and then got up. "I'm going down to the Wildlife Preserve. Can you fix me a couple of sandwiches?"

"Just a moment," said his mother. He stood still, unwillingly. "Your father is worn out right now with his work—just as I'm worn out with the baby. But you're big enough to take a little of the family responsibility on your own shoulders, for a short while anyway. The launch will be over soon and your father did say he might have a pleasant surprise for us all then. Surely you can take care of a few things, including yourself, until that time comes."

"Well, sure," growled Rolf.

"All right, then. You can begin by making your own sandwiches and clean up the breakfast table." With that, Mrs. Gunnarson walked out of the kitchen.

Rolf cleared the table and put the dishes in the washer. Then he made up four sandwiches, took a plastic bottle of orange juice, and stuffed them all into the little knapsack on the back of his bike's seat. He whistled for Mr. Sheperton and pedaled down the street to Rita's house. She was already sitting on the shady porch in front of the old house.

"Want to meet Lugh?" Rolf asked her, straddling his bike at the base of the front steps.

Rita's eyes widened. "Could I?"

"Sure."

She leaped off her chair and ran into the house. In two minutes flat she was out again, holding a little lunchkit in one hand.

Together they biked down toward Playa-linda Beach, with Mr. Sheperton gallumphing alongside them and the sea breeze pushing fluffy white clouds across the bright blue sky. It was like old times, before the launch and the gremlins made Rolf's life so complicated.

Except that Mr. Sheperton didn't say a word to Rolf all the way down toward the beach. He didn't even bark. And he stayed alongside Rita's bike, on the side away from Rolf.

He's sore at me, Rolf realized.

"That time you hurt your leg diving off the high board," Rita called to him, raising her voice enough to be heard over the whistling wind, "why did you try that dive? You'd never been off the high board before."

Rolf shrugged. "I had to show people.

The other guys were calling me chicken . . . "

"No they weren't," Rita said. "I was there and I heard them. There was a lot of horsing around going on, but nobody called you chicken."

He could feel his face getting red. "Well—I guess I was getting sore at them for showing

off in front of you girls. I didn't want to be left out. They were always calling me the runt and bugging me. And you were watching them, and I didn't want you to think I was chicken. . . ."

"Oh, Rolf," she said, shaking her head. "Boys are so silly. Why would I think you're chicken? I've known you all my life; I know you're not chicken. A little silly sometimes, maybe . . ."

She laughed, and Rolf found that he was laughing with her.

"I guess I just wanted you to think that I was as big as any of the guys. As important as any of them."

Her face grew serious again. "Is that why you're helping the gremlins? So that they'll help you feel important?"

"Yeah . . . no . . ." Rolf felt confused. "Aw, I don't know. I'm not even sure how I got into this."

Baneen did not meet them before they got to the Hollow, as usual. In fact they came into the very Hollow itself before any sort of attention was paid them by the gremlins. When they reached the lip of the hollow they saw why. All work seemed to be at a standstill, with all the gremlins watching one corner of the Hollow that seemed to be obscured by a cloud of green smoke. Curious, Rolf went toward the smoke, with Rita and Mr. Sheperton behind him, and as he got close, he heard voices coming from it. Specifically, he heard Baneen's voice, on a high sarcastic note.

" . . . Ah, round is it, indeed? A round universe?" Baneen was saying. "And what happens to magic when you're on the underside of it, may I ask now? It's all upside-down is it? And all the spells backward?"

"Not so!" hissed the voice O'Rigami—and Rolf with Rita and Mr. Sheperton pushed through the green smoke to find a clear space within which O'Rigami and Baneen were confronting each other, with perhaps six feet of distance between them. "Being round, all praces on universe identicar. Sperrs arways the same!"

"Ah, dear me, and do you really believe such nonsense?" demanded Baneen, still sarcastically. "It's a fever you must be having, for certain. I've noticed you're not looking yourself, nowadays—"

As he spoke, he passed his hands one over the other and O'Rigami turned from his normal gremlin green color to a bright reddish brown plaid in color.

"Am in perfect shape and coror!" snapped O'Rigami, turning sharply back to green. His fingers twinkled and a piece of paper which had appeared from nowhere suddenly took on the shape of a miniature garden fountain. "Also happen to understand more of universe than others who might stirr be too ignorant—"

The fountain suddenly spouted a fine stream of water which arched up through the air forward and curved down again abruptly to splatter Baneen generously behind his pointed gremlin ears.

Baneen yelped and dodged. Suddenly he

turned into a crocodile which charged at O'Rigami, jaws agape, drinking up the water from the fountain as it came.

O'Rigami's flying fingers abruptly fashioned a Spanish bullfighter's cape with which he executed perfectly that pass with the cape known as a veronica. Completely fooled by the cape, the crocodile thundered past, discovered itself facing nothing, and whirled about. But O'Rigami had already folded a complete stony medieval castle about himself and was hidden in it.

The crocodile turned abruptly into a gopher, which leaped forward and began to tunnel into the earth out of sight and toward the castle. The castle arose on two thin green legs and scurried aside. It unfolded and disappeared suddenly, revealing O'Rigami, whose flying fingers wove a fisherman's net in the air where the castle had originally been.

The gopher popped up through the earth where the castle had been. The net fell about it in folds, entangling it. And abruptly the gopher turned back into Baneen, trapped in the netting.

"Help!" cried the little gremlin. "Help. O'Rigami, help now! Turn me loose!"

"Onry," said O'Rigami, sternly, "on condition you wirr not insist any more on this nonsense about the universe being frat!"

"I promise. Indeed, I promise!" cried Baneen. "Word of Baneen!"

"No, you don't!" said O'Rigami. "This is fourteen thousand, five hundred and ereventh time you've brought up same argument. I don't want to argue it with you ever again. Give me your gremrinish word—or you stay in that net for the next million years!"

"Ah, no!" begged Baneen. "Not that! O'Rigami, friend of me youth—"

"Your gremrinish word, or there you stay!" said O'Rigami implacably, folding his arms.

Baneen sighed and drooped inside the net.

"All right," he said, sulkily. "My gremlinish word—I'll agree the universe is round from now on!"

O'Rigami waved his hands and the net vanished. Baneen climbed to his feet and brushed himself off. But his face was sulky.

"Ah," he said, "but it's a terrible thing, it is, for one true gremlin to require the Unbreakable Promise from another. Bad dreams to your cruel mind, O'Rigami, and may your conscience prick you that did such to an old friend—"

Just then he became aware of Rolf and the others watching, and his sulky look was transformed into a smile.

"But here's the lad and the lass as well, to say nothing of Mr. Sheperton!" Baneen exclaimed. "Welcome to our humble abode, fairest of lasses. It's pleased we are that you've come to visit with us."

Rita's eyes sparkled like a child's on Christmas morning. "How did you know I was coming here? I mean, you weren't surprised to see me at all, were you?"

"Of course not. Gremlins can foresee the future, you know—er, only on special occasions, such as this one, that is. And only up to a limited point, don't you know."

"Foresee the future?" Rita asked. "Can you . . ."

"Ah, but it's not my chatter you've come for, is it?" Baneen said. "You've come to meet our masterful and baleful leader, Lugh of the Long Hand, Prince of the Royal House of Gremla."

Rita laughed, delighted. "He knows everything!"

But Rolf, somehow, was feeling much less than happy. Baneen led Rita into the misty-aired Hollow and Rolf fell into step behind them.

Mr. Sheperton, walking beside Rolf, muttered, "Trust a gremlin to flatter a human straight out of his—or her—senses." But he seemed to be saying it more to himself than to Rolf.

Baneen was saying, as they went through the Hollow, "Lugh's not here at the present moment. He's out watching those scalawag poachers in their great oily boat."

"They're back again?" Rolf asked.

"Sure enough. That squeaky-voiced captain and his two ugly sailors have brought a few businessmen with them this time. He's showing them what a grand view they're going to have of the launch. And promising them roast wild duck for their dinners! Lugh's there at the beach, protecting them from being spotted by the rangers. And boiling in his own juices if I know Lugh the Terrible-Tempered."

"Hmph," said Mr. Sheperton.

"So I'd be advising you," Baneen continued, "to be careful of not being seen by the poachers. And be even more careful of not triggering the wrath of Lugh. He'll be in a foul mood, no doubt. Making magic on a continuous basis for several hours is a terrible strain, especially next to all that water, you know."

Lugh did look terribly strained when they saw him. And angrier than ever. He was standing atop a high dune that overlooked the beach, his cheeks puffed out, his face red, his fists clenched at his sides. From time to time, as a breeze puffed in from the sea, he would actually float off the sand a few inches, like a baloon, and then settle down again slowly.

Baneen called to him when they got near enough. "Lugh, me magic-making marvel, I've brought you some visitors to help pass away the morning."

Turning, Lugh gruffed, "Visitors, is it? I'll

thank you, tricky one, to watch those smelly, water-crawling spalpeens for a while."

"Nothing could please me more, Lugh darling," Baneen said happily, "than to give you a bit of rest from your mighty labors. I'll take care of the scalawags for you."

And Baneen planted himself on the dune's crest, puffed out his cheeks, squeezed his fists until the knuckles went chartreuse, and put on a glowering scowl just like Lugh's.

"Ahhh..." said Lugh. "I feel better already. You'll be the lass Baneen told me of. You've come to help this lad here?"

"Well," Rita said, sitting on the sand, "I suppose so...."

"Hah. And a good thing it is that you have. It's almost time for us to leave this foulsome planet, and we'll be needing all the help we can muster."

"It's not a foulsome planet!" Rita snapped. "It's a beautiful planet."

Lugh glared at her. "Is it now? Well, maybe once it was, when we first came here, but not today. Not when you've got ugly ones like those down in the boat dirtying up the very air we breathe with their smelly engines and oily garbage."

"Well, you're helping them!" Rita said. "You're protecting them. Why don't you use some of your gremlin magic to chase them away?"

Rolf watched her, goggle-eyed. Any minute now, he knew, Lugh was going to explode and turn her into a tree stump. He reached out for Rita's arm.

But Lugh's answer was strangely soft, quiet, even sad. "Ah, lass, but it's not our world. It belongs to you humans—it's the world you made for yourselves, in a manner of speaking. Once we thought that we might help you, if you had the will to handle matters right—but it turned out to be of no use, no use at all."

He stalked away, moodily.

"What does he mean?" Rita demanded of Baneen.

The little gremlin shook his head, but without taking his eyes off the men he was supposed to be watching.

"It's a sad tale, indeed," he said. "And a specially sad tale in the part of it that concerns Lugh, himself. It was his idea, you see, to disguise the Great Corkscrew and use it as a test to find one human who cared more for others than himself. And when no such human could be found, it was Lugh that took it the hardest of us all—though never a sign would he show of how he felt."

"No such human could be found?" Rolf echoed. "Surely there've been lots of humans who cared more for others than themselves?"

"Oh, indeed, there have been—but it was for other *humans* they cared. Never yet has a human been found who cares more for other

creatures than he or she does for himself or herself."

"But how would a corkscrew show the difference—" Rita began.

"Ah, but it's not just any corkscrew!" said Baneen, swiftly. "It's the Great Corkscrew of Gremla, that symbol of Gremlin kingship that belonged to Hamrod the Heartless and which Lugh himself stole away from the king when he brought us here—to pay Hamrod back for all his pranks and tricks upon Lugh, himself. You see, in olden days—so far back that your world of Earth was still a steaming mudball, cooling down into a planet—the Great Corkscrew was a test of Gremlin kingship. Only one wielding more power and magic than any other gremlin could pull it from its case. He who could withdraw the Corkscrew was rightwise king of all Gremla. Every thousand years or so, whoever was our Gremlin king must pull forth the Corkscrew to prove his right to rule."

Baneen paused and sighed heavily.

"If at that time he could not pull it out," he went on, "then all other gremlins who wished to try had their chance—until one succeeded and gained the throne. Ah, but the sad year came, and the sad month and the sad day—the then king of Gremla not having been able to pull out the corkscrew— when every other gremlin on Gremla had tried as well, and none had been able."

"None?" said Rolf. "One of them must have had a little stronger magic than any of the rest. It just had to be."

Baneen shook his head.

"No, lad," he said. "It's clear you don't understand the strange and marvelous principles of magic. It's not how strong your magic is, but how much of it you have. The greater your soul, the more magic you can carry. And over the centuries, unbeknownst to ourselves, our gremlin souls had become smaller and smaller, so that even the largest soul among us could not hold enough magic to let its owner pull the Great Corkscrew from its case."

"But," said Rita, "if nobody could pull the Great Corkscrew out, what happened to the kingship?"

Baneen shrugged.

"Indeed, what could happen?" he said. "Since no one could pull the Corkscrew forth, it fell into disuse as a test of king-worthiness. The then king stayed on the throne, and those who came after him were smaller and smaller of soul until at the end, Hamrod the Heartless was rumored to have none at all — and sure his actions seemed to testify to that. But still it was said, that secretly Hamrod would go and pull at the Corkscrew now and then to try and prove himself rightful king. It was to deprive him of that hope of kingship-proof that Lugh stole the Cork-screw away and brought it here."

"What's all this about using the thing as a test, then?" growled Mr. Sheperton. "If no one could pull it out, what was the use of it?"

"Ah, but it was only no *gremlin* who could pull it out!" said Baneen. "That did not mean there was no human about with a soul large enough to free it. Indeed, Lugh's conscience had been troubling him for some time then about our gremlin rights on this world of yours and whether it had not become our world—a second Gremla, as it were—just by our being here so long. He decided that we would change our age-old custom of keeping to ourselves, and follow humans, if only humans could prove themselves worthy of being followed. So, to find out if such proof was possible, he set up a legend and a place, and disguised the Corkscrew itself so that no one could guess its origin, and then waited for what would happen."

"What did happen?" asked Rolf.

"Do you need to ask, Rolf?" demanded Mr. Sheperton. "Isn't it clear the rascal's trying to make us believe that the celebrated sword in the stone of Arthurian legend was no other than his gremlin Corkscrew?"

"And so it was," Baneen nodded.

"Stuff and nonsense!" snorted Mr. Sheperton. "Corkscrew indeed! It was a sword!"

"But—" said Rolf. "King Arthur pulled the sword out of the stone and was crowned king of England because of it—"

"So he did and was. But it was only with gremlin aid he was able to pull the blade forth—though little he suspected that, himself." said Baneen. "It happened that by the time young Arthur got his chance to try pulling loose the sword nearly everyone in England who stood a likelihood of being accepted king, if he did pull it forth, had tried and failed. Now, Arthur was very great of soul—but not quite great enough by the width of a dragonfly's wing, as all we gremlins know. So it happened that a number of us went and pleaded with Lugh, and Lugh consented to our getting invisibly within the stone to push, while Arthur pulled—and so the sword came forth."

"Hurrah!" cheered Mr. Sheperton.

"Ah, but if you remember, it all turned out sadly," said Baneen. "Arthur prospered for a while, and brought justice to his kingdom. But you remember how his reign ended—the knights of the Round Table all divided against themselves, with Lancelot on one side and Arthur on the other, so that everything fell back to savagery and barbarism again."

There was a moment's silence.

"I'd like to try pulling that Corkscrew out," said Rolf, thoughtfully.

Baneen had been doing all this talking while keeping his eye on the boat and his fists clenched at his sides. In the process he had gradually drifted upward off the ground. He reached down now with one hand to make a brief pass in the air before Rolf. There was a shimmer and something took shape. It was not easy to see it clearly, but it was something like a massive bone handle attached to something metallic that was wrapped and sheathed in light.

"Try it, indeed, lad," said Baneen, heavily. "It can do no harm—though no good, either."

Rolf hesitated a second, then took hold of the handle with both hands and pulled. He strained, but the handle did not move.

"You see?" said Baneen wistfully. He waved his hand and the Great Corkscrew faded once more from sight. "Had you been able to pull it forth, you could have called on the House of Lugh of the Long Hand, and on Lugh himself, for any single thing you wished— for so did Lugh swear, giving his gremlinish word, back before Arthur was crowned king. But as you see, you cannot do it—no human nor gremlin can, these days. And that was why, when Arthur failed, Lugh determined that there was no hope for us in humans, and we must all return to Gremla. So we are, indeed, now, as you know—*Gremla save me!*"

The last words came out in a yelp; and

from beyond the dune they suddenly heard several men's voices yelling at once. Rolf looked up at Baneen and saw the little gremlin now floating nearly a dozen feet off the ground, drifting like a soap bubble in the breeze, his tiny arms folded across his chest, his face still scowling mightily.

"What? What's all this?" barked Mr. Sheperton.

The yelling voices were coming from the boat. In the distance, the voice of Lugh bellowed, "Baneen, you wart-toad, get down there!" Rolf sprinted up to the top of the dune. He flattened out on his belly and motioned to Rita to do the same. She did, right beside him, and they both peered carefully through the tall grass.

The poachers' boat was a mess. A tall geyser of water was sprouting amidships, and the engine in the stern was boiling off a huge cloud of smoke. The sailors were scampering around the deck, plainly not knowing what to do first.

The captain was screeching, "She's sinking! She's sinking!"

Two men in business suits and sunglasses were looking pale and frightened. They were up at the prow of the boat, their mouths open.

"Help!" came Baneen's voice from high above, as suddenly the geyser of water shifted its angle until it began dousing the businessmen. They spluttered noisily and waved their arms, trying to ward off the liquid showering down on them.

"I said *get down!*" Lugh roared. He was back on the scene now, looking up at Baneen.

Baneen made some twisting motions, paddling his feet in midair. He cried out helplessly: "By the Sacred Stone of Gremla, I've used up so much magic on those scalawags that I can't get down again!"

Lugh's face looked like a thundercloud. "Let the spalpeen hang there 'til sundown, then," he muttered. And he stalked off, heading back for the Gremlin Hollow.

Rolf lay there in the sand, turning to watch the furious activity in the boat, which was still leaking and smoking. Then he looked up at Baneen again.

The little gremlin seemed genuinely frightened. "Lugh, me darling, don't leave me here, please! The wind's shifting . . . see, I'm blowing out to sea. You wouldn't have me land in a watery grave would you, Lugh, oh most handsome and powerful of gremlins . . . would you, Lugh . . . would you?" Baneen's voice got higher with each word. And sure enough, he was starting to drift toward the crest of the sand dune, heading toward the ocean.

Lugh stopped and looked back up at Baneen. "A watery grave it is for you, trickster. You've gotten yourself into this predicament with your tricks; now see if you can get yourself out. I'll not help you."

"Water's bad for gremlins," Rolf said to Rita.

"It could be very bad for Baneen if he falls into the ocean," Mr. Sheperton admitted grudgingly. "Gremlins are immortal, of course, but still—"

"Look," Rolf pointed. "He's drifting over this way. Maybe we can grab him when he comes up to the top of the dune."

"The people from the boat will see us," Mr. Sheperton said.

"They've got enough troubles right now," Rolf answered quickly, glancing at the still-frantic action on the boat. "They won't be looking this way. And besides, we can't just let Baneen float away without trying to help."

Mr. Sheperton gazed for a long moment at Baneen's flailing form, floating slowly toward them. "He's too high," the dog said with a shake of his shaggy head. "I can't jump that high."

Rita nodded. "I'm afraid he's right, Rolf. We can't reach him, even from the crest of the dune."

Rolf could feel his face settle into a stubborn frown. "Oh, yeah? Well, we're not going to sit here and let him go out to sea without at least trying to help."

He got to his feet and walked slowly down toward the bottom of the dune. About halfway down, Rolf looked up, checked Baneen's position, then started trotting along the dune's slope to get exactly under the gremlin. He waited a few moments, letting Baneen drift closer to the top of the dune.

Then Rolf started running. He sprinted up the slope of the dune, toward the crest, stride, stride, each stride longer than the one before it. Baneen was already at the crest and starting to drift past when Rolf hit the top and leaped!

His outstretched fingers wrapped around one of Baneen's feet. Rolf hit the sand with a thud and sprawled over on his face, with the yowling, yelping Baneen safely in one hand.

"What's that?" yelled the man in the suit.

Rolf had landed on the seaward side of the dune. Mr. Sheperton dashed out and picked up Baneen in his teeth, while Rita came over to help Rolf to his feet.

"It's that kid and the dog again!" the captain squeaked. "After them, and this time I want them brought back here!"

All five of them, the two drenched businessmen, the two grimy sailors, and the captain scrambled out of the boat and toward Rolf and his friends.

Rolf started back for the dune's crest, holding Rita by one arm. But at the top, he saw Lugh, standing there with his legs straddled wide and his arms folded against his chest.

"You're a brave lad," Lugh said sternly.

"Don't worry about those spalpeens."

Lugh gave a fierce glance, then pointed one finger at the advancing five men. *"May the Wrath of Gremla strike your heads."*

Rolf turned to watch.

Immediately, a rain of bottles, cigarette butts, beer cans, wadded-up paper, plastic cups, a thousand and one items fell out of the empty air onto the heads of the approaching men. They yelled and screamed, flung their arms over their heads, tripped and sprawled on the sand as bottle after bottle, can after can, ashtrays, paper plates, a cloudburst of junk fell upon them.

Lugh smiled grimly. "They've been tossing those things out of their nasty boat for weeks, they have. And I've been saving it all for them."

Rolf stared, amazed, as the five men staggered and limped back under the safety of their camouflaged bridge. The trash kept pouring down on them until they were all under protection. Magically, none of the trash littered the beach. It was all clean.

Rolf's last glimpse of the men, as he and Rita went over behind the sand dune's shoulder, showed him all five of them cowering under the bridge, trembling and wide-eyed. Even the captain was stained with dirt and sweat, and his beautiful jacket was covered with sand.

As they walked back to the Gremlin Hollow,

with Lugh several paces ahead of the rest, Baneen began to prance around as spryly as ever.

"Ah, you saved me, lad. Saved me from a fate worse than death . . . water." The little gremlin shuddered.

"It was awfully brave of you," Rita agreed.

Rolf fluttered his hands in embarrassment.

"And such a leap!" Baneen went on. "Like an Olympian the boy jumped. And here I thought you had a bad leg, me bucko. Could it be all healed now?"

Rolf had forgotten about his bad leg. "Yeah . . . " he said, feeling a strange glow inside. "I guess it *is* all healed."

"Ah, you see?" Baneen said, turning to Mr. Sheperton. "The lad's dealings with gremlins hasn't been all that bad for him, now has it? We cured his leg without half trying."

Mr. Sheperton huffed, "Typical gremlin chicanery. Don't take credit, Baneen, for Rolf's good health. His leg mended on its own. He just hadn't tested it until today. You had nothing to do with the healing of it."

"Perhaps, perhaps. But the lad still *thought* his leg was weak, until I arranged to show him otherwise."

"You arranged?" Rolf said, thunderstruck.

"Ah, well, it was really nothing . . . nothing at all," said the little gremlin, carelessly. "And it did my heart good to see those scalawags running about in the sinking boat.

Let's talk of more interesting things—"

"No, you don't!" barked Mr. Sheperton. "We've had enough of your sneaky gremlin hint-and-slip-away. Let's have the matter straight, for once. Rolf, Baneen was only having fun at the expense of the people in the boat. There was never a thought in that tiny brain of his about your leg until after it was all over. Don't let him try to pretend otherwise."

"Oh, to be sure, and it's the grand, wise dog you are, to be saying what was in my mind and what was not!" cried Baneen. "Had enough of our gremlin ways, you say—and did it ever cross your mind we'd have become a bit tired of your grump, grump, grumping doggish ways, all the time? Sure it's more than green flesh and blood can take, your everlasting criticism and belittling of our gremlin doings and all things gremlinish!"

"Wait a minute," said Rolf hastily. Neither Baneen nor the dog, however, were listening.

"Want to have it out, do you?" Mr. Sheperton snarled. "Come on, then! Called a spade a spade ever since I was a pup—I'll call a gremlin a gremlin to my dying day. If you don't like it—" He bared his teeth.

Baneen shot up in the air out of the dog's reach and hung there, vibrating with indignation.

"You and your great fangs!" he cried.
"Thinking you can get away with anything.
But beware, dog—we gremlins are not unprotected. Push me but one small push more,
and I'll call forth a dragon to crunch and
munch and slay you!"

"Hah!" snorted Mr. Sheperton. "Call forth
a dragon, indeed! Enough of your rascally
tall tales!"

"'Tis no tall tale!" shouted Baneen, almost dancing in the air with rage. "As you
may find out to your cost, unless you mend
your ways!"

"Come, come! A dragon? What sort of
fool do you take me for? If you've got a
dragon, let's see it!"

"Woe to you, if I call him forth!"

"Woe me not, gremlin! I said, produce
this dragon or admit you've not got him."

"You'll rue that word, Mr. Sheperton—"

"Just as I thought!" snorted the dog
disgustedly. "There's no such thing as a
dragon around you gremlins."

"No such—!" screeched Baneen.

"That's what I said."

"No DRAGON?"

"None!"

"Dog, it's too far you've gone this day—"

"Wait. Wait—" said Rolf, hastily. "Look,
there's no need for the two of you to get all
geared up about this. Baneen, why don't you
just give Mr. Sheperton your gremlinish word

the dragon exists. Then—"

"Gremlinish word?" Baneen swallowed suddenly and looked unhappy. "Guk—"

"AND WHAT'S ALL THIS ABOUT GREMLINISH WORDS?" thundered a familiar voice. Lugh stalked into the midst of them.

"Ah . . . Lugh, darling, are you sure you heard the lad just right, now?" stammered Baneen. "Was it really the word grem—"

"I heard what I heard, and well you know I heard it." scowled Lugh. "What's all this talk about the Unbreakable Promise—and by humans and dogs, at that?"

"Not about to have my intelligence insulted!" huffed Mr. Sheperton. "Your green friend here was just threatening me with a dragon."

"And I," said Rolf, still trying to pour oil on the troubled waters, "just suggested that Baneen give Mr. Sheperton his . . . er . . . gremlinish word that the dragon existed, and let that settle the matter."

Lugh's scowl grew even blacker.

"Where did you hear about the gremlinish word, boy?" he demanded.

"Why, just the other time I was here," said Rolf, "Baneen and O'Rigami were having a little argument about the shape of the universe—"

"So!" Lugh swung on Baneen, fixing him with a fiery eye. The smaller gremlin slid apologetically down out of the air to the ground. "You let slip that there's a promise no gremlin can ever break, did you, me noisy chatterer? And now you've let your tongue run away with you about our gremlin dragon? Very well, we'll let this be a lesson to you. You've threatened the dog with the dragon. Now, produce it!"

"Ah, sure, and so much isn't needful, surely—" began Baneen.

"PRODUCE IT!"

"Wait!" Rolf swallowed hard. "You mean there really is—" He put his arms protectively around Mr. Sheperton's neck. "You're not going to sic any dragon on my dog—"

"Let it come," snarled Mr. Sheperton, raking the ground with his forepaws. "By St. George, I'll meet the creature tooth to tooth and nail to nail!"

"Shep, be quiet, won't you?" said Rolf desperately. "Lugh—" Lugh was standing with his arms folded, staring at Baneen, who was unhappily making passes in the air with his hands. Around the Hollow, all the other gremlins had fallen silent and were standing, watching. A puff of red smoke billowed up between Baneen's hands, and the little gremlin jumped back.

Rolf shoved himself hastily in front of Mr. Sheperton, facing the smoke.

"Wait!" he cried. "If anything happens to Shep I won't lift a hand to help you get your kite—"

"Too late," said Lugh, grimly.

The red smoke thinned—revealing not a large and fearsome creature with scales and fiery breath, but a small round table with a green tablecloth and a small white structure, something like a bird house, sitting in the middle of it.

"What?" said Rolf, staring at it.

"Baneen!" snapped Lugh commandingly. Baneen gulped and turned toward the little house.

"Mighty dragon of mighty Gremla!" he piped. "Come forth! Come forth and slay!"

From the dark doorway of the birdhouse came a small puff of smoke, then nothing for a few seconds, then another puff of smoke. Finally a third puff of smoke appeared with a tiny flicker of yellow flame in the midst of it.

"*Come forth,* dragon!" cried Baneen, in a high, desperate voice. "We command you!"

A tiny green dragon-head poked itself out of the opening, looked around, sighed heavily and withdrew. There was a metallic rattling sound inside the bird house, another sigh, and a small voice squeaked thinly. "Slay! Slay!"

The dragon came dancing out of the bird house on to the table, a minuscule sword in each of its front paws.

"Slay! Slay!" it cried, making threatening

gestures all around with the swords and puffing out small round puffs of smoke with an occasional flicker of flame in them. "Slay! Slay . . . slay . . . sl . . . "

The dragon began to pant. The flame disappeared entirely and the puffs of smoke themselves grew thin. The swords it held began to droop.

" . . . Slay . . . " the dragon wheezed. It looked appealingly at Baneen. "Slay . . . how much . . . longer? I'm . . . slay . . . not as young as I . . . slay . . . used to be, you know. . . . "

"Enough!" said Lugh abruptly with a wave of his hand. "Back into your house and rest easy. The word of Lugh of the Long Hand is that you won't be called on for at least another ten thousand years."

"Huff . . . thank you . . . sir . . . " panted the dragon. It withdrew into its house; and house, table and all, disappeared in another puff of green smoke.

"Back to work, all the rest of you." The other gremlins returned to their activities.

"Let that settle the matter, then!" snapped Lugh. Lugh stalked off. Rolf, Rita, and Mr. Sheperton were left facing a crestfallen Baneen.

"Well, well," grumped the dog in a curiously apologetic tone of voice. "Didn't mean to put you on the spot, Baneen, old man. Didn't really believe you had a dragon. Apologies, I'm sure."

"Ah, now, and that's kind of you, Mr. Sheperton," said Baneen, sadly. "But that great monster Lugh had the right of it. It was me own fault for threatening you with the poor creature. Sure, and my tongue clean ran away with me."

"Say no more," gruffed Mr. Sheperton.

"But it was a full-sized dragon, once, indeed it was," said Baneen, looking appealingly at the dog and the two humans alike. "Back on bright and dusty Gremla. The personal dragon of the House of Lugh, full twenty cubits in height and forty-six cubits long. However, it was necessary to shrink it down a bit in order to bring it to this Earth of yours; and as I've mentioned before—the watery place that it is here, not even Lugh could grow the creature back to its proper size again—not that we'd have wanted to risk letting it run around loose and maybe get killed off, like all your native dragons were, back in the days of the knights. Ah, it's cruel they were to the native dragons, your iron ancestors, murdering them on sight; and all in the name of honor and glory."

Baneen sighed heavily. Rolf found himself sighing right along with the small gremlin. A few dragons, still alive, could have made modern life much more interesting.

9

"What was it Baneen and the other gremlin—" began Rita as they were cycling home.

"O'Rigami," said Rolf. "He's the Grand Engineer."

"Oh?" Rita said. "What were he and Baneen talking to you about just before we left?"

"The blueprints," said Rolf, still deep in his own thoughts. "I don't know why they can't steal their own blueprints instead of leaving it up to me for everything."

"They want you to steal a blueprint?" cried Rita. "A blueprint of what?"

"Of the spacecraft's life-support system," Rolf answered. "I told them I couldn't. Even if I could get into Dad's office and even if the blueprints were there for me to find, I wouldn't recognize which one was the right one even if I saw it. I'm going to get them a poster, instead."

"A poster?"

"Sure," Rolf glanced at her as he pedaled. "You remember that wall-poster I got out at the Cape Kennedy Visitor's Center last May? The one with the chart on the back of what the spacecraft controls look like."

"But that's not the same thing as a blueprint," Rita said.

"I know, but for gremlins it doesn't make much difference, I guess." Rolf thought back to the way O'Rigami had explained it all to him. "It's only necessary for O'Rigami to touch the Speciar Virtue—"

"The what?" asked Rita.

"The Speciar Virtue . . ."

"You sound like you've got a Japanese accent."

"It's a gremlin accent," said Rolf, gloomily. "One of them, anyway. I meant the Spe*cial* Virtue of an object. O'Rigami says that all he needs to do is touch the Special Virtue of the spacecraft to the Magical Device—the space kite, that is. I'm just hoping that there's the right Special Virtue in my poster." He shook his head. "Gremlin magic doesn't work the way our science does."

Rita said, "I don't understand it."

"Neither do I," admitted Rolf. "Anyway, I hope the poster works as well as the blueprints for O'Rigami. But that's the easy part. It's getting up on the launch tower that worries me. I've got to do that tonight."

Mr. Sheperton, who had been trotting along between the two bikes, muttered, "Tomfoolery, all this gremlin nonsense."

Rolf frowned at the dog, then looked back at Rita. "That's why you've got to help me."

"Me?"

"Well," said Rolf. "I can't get into the Space Center and up to the launch tower all by myself. Your dad checks the men on the gates every night. If you went there because you wanted to talk to him, I was thinking maybe you could keep his attention while I sneaked in—"

"Rolf!" Rita was clearly upset. "I couldn't do that."

"Then we're done for."

"Not we. *You*," said Rita, a little coldly.

"I mean all of us, the gremlins, the space program, everything."

Rita stared at him again. He could feel her eyes searching through him as he pedaled straight down the road, toward the setting sun.

"Why do you say the space program and . . . everything?" she asked at last.

"Because," he said, looking at her again, "I think Lugh can really keep the rocket from going up, if he wants to. Dad's always talking about the millions of parts in every rocket and how each one has to work just right. If Lugh can stop just a few of them, important ones, from working, nothing would happen. Or the whole rocket might blow up!"

"He wouldn't do that! Would he?"

Rolf shrugged. "He's got some temper. I saw him demolish a bulldozer—zowie! Just like that."

Rita nodded her head. "If the rocket doesn't go up—or blows up—that would cause trouble for the whole space program, all right."

"You know it," said Rolf.

"I . . . well, what good is it going to do, your getting up in the launch tower?"

"I've got to attach the kite onto the spacecraft," Rolf said.

Rita said nothing for a long moment.

"I don't know . . ." she said. "Why did you start out helping them, in the first place?"

She stared penetratingly at him. He rode along for a few seconds, scowling at the road.

"Baneen told me I could have a Great Wish—the same sort of thing I guess you get if you pull their Corkscrew out of its case. I asked them to clean up all the pollution and make the ecology safe and he gave me the word of Baneen they would, just as soon as I'd helped them."

"Did you ask for his gremlinish word?" Rita asked.

Rolf shook his head.

"I didn't know about gremlinish words then," he said. "I suppose I should have."

"You'd better now."

"I guess. Only . . ." he hesitated. "You know, the more I think of it, the more I think the gremlins just can't do it. Maybe I should have suspected when Baneen agreed just like that."

"Can't do it?" She was watching him as they rode along.

"Not really," he growled. "How can they? Cleaning up all the pollution in the world is too big a job, for one thing. And even if they could clean it up, how could they protect the environment from now on without staying on the job to protect it? In fact, if they could do all that, how come they haven't done it before on their own?"

He shook his head.

"No," he said, "the more I think of it, the only way anything that big can be done would be with all humans and all gremlins working together."

"Then that's what you want to ask for," said Rita.

"How can I?" he said. "I can't make them promise to stay here as the price for my helping them get away. They can't do both things at the same time."

"Rolf," she said suddenly and energetically, "you don't make any sense at all! If this is the way you feel, how come you're helping them leave at all?"

He shrugged.

"I guess . . . " he said, slowly, "I guess it's because I suppose they've got a right to go home—just like the animals here in the Preserve have got a right to live without being hunted and the brown pelicans have got a right not to have the shells of their eggs weakened by DDT pollution."

They rode along in silence for a little while.

"It's all right," said Rita after a while. "I'll help you."

Rolf lifted his head.

"Great," he said.

"Terrible!" groused Mr. Sheperton.

At seven-thirty that night, Rolf and Shep, stood just outside the Gate Number Twelve of the Space Center. Rolf straddled his bike as Baneen floated a few feet off the ground beside him. They were all invisible—even Rolf's bike.

" . . . and what I don't see," Rolf was saying to Baneen, "is why you can't keep me invisible once I'm past the gate. If you'd just go in with me."

"Lad, lad," said Baneen sadly, "sure, and how am I to explain to you the terrible mysteries and such of gremlin magic, the same which has taken millions of years for gremlins to develop and you'd want an answer to every question about it that comes to mind!"

"Terrible . . ." muttered Shep, trailing off to something too low to be understood.

"As a matter of fact," said Baneen, "there's a metal cable underneath the road at the gate, with enough iron to keep a gremlin out. For a gremlin to cross cold iron is sort of like a human getting an electric shock. It's terribly hurtful."

"You could go around the gate," said Rolf.

"Well, now, there's bits and things of iron—or steel, if you will have it—all over the Space Center, no telling when a gremlin might run into it; and it's all most uncomfortable. Which is why, eager as we all are to see the fair, cloudless skies of Gremla, once more, it's been decided we wait safely in our Hollow until launch time and then magic ourselves directly to the safety of the space kite you'll have fixed to the rocket by then. . . ."

He broke off abruptly. Rita had just come riding down the road out of the darkness into the lights of the gate and dismounted to speak to the gate guard.

"Hi, Tom." Her voice came clearly to their ears from less than thirty feet away. "Has my dad been by yet?"

"Not yet, Rita," the guard said. "What is it?"

"Oh, nothing—I just wanted to ask him about having one of my girl friends stay over next weekend. Her folks are going out of town. . . . " Rita chattered on.

"What a fine lass she is, to be sure," said Baneen, fondly.

"Indeed she is!" snapped Shep. "No thanks to corrupting gremlin influences!"

"Now, is that a nice thing to say—" Baneen broke off again. A white Space Center security car was wheeling up to the inside of the gate. It stopped and Rita's father got out.

"Rita!" he said. "What are you doing here?"

He walked over to the gate, toward the guard and his daughter.

"Dad, Mom said to ask you," Rita said, energetically. "You know Ginny Magruder? Well, her folks are going over to New Orleans for three days, for a wedding of her cousin, and Ginny doesn't want to go, because it'll be nothing but older people and she doesn't like those cousins, anyway. So I said, why not come and spend the weekend with me; and she was really happy—you should have seen her. So, she said she'd have to ask her own folks, and she did and they said yes—"

"Off you go, lad!" hissed Baneen. "Now, whilst they're both still listening to her. The dog and I will meet you back here in an hour and a half."

"Don't know why I couldn't—" Shep began to grumble.

"No. Stay," said Rolf. He did not want to worry about anyone but himself on a trip like this. He hopped on his bike; and then remembered something.

He turned to Baneen.

"I don't have the space kite yet—"

"Go, lad! Go!" whispered Baneen, giving his bike a shove, that—light as it was—started the wheels rolling, so that Rolf's feet went automatically to the pedals.

"Look in your hip pocket when you get to the rocket!" he heard Baneen whisper behind him. Then he was past the gate and suddenly visible.

But the backs of both the guard and Rita's father were to him. Furiously, he began to pedal off down the road toward the tall, spotlighted shape of the distant rocket, illuminated according to custom, this night before the launch.

Gate Twelve was the closest of all the entrances to the Space Center to the launch pad of the rocket. But it was still several miles away; and it took Rolf some twenty minutes of hard pedaling to reach it. As he came close to the floodlighted area, he slowed down and finally stopped, just outside the lights that were making the pad and the rocket itself almost daylight-bright. He hid his bike in the brush just off the road and moved slowly up behind one of the lights in the darkest shadow behind it. Hidden in

that shadow, he studied the launch area for evidence of guards.

There *had* to be guards, he thought—and there were. After some minutes of watching he located two of them: one, sitting in one of the white, security sedans and another making a regular round of the pad and the rocket, up along the top of the launch pad itself. As he watched, the security sedan started up and drove off, taking one of the guards away.

The other guard was now around the far side of the launch pad, as out of sight of Rolf, as Rolf was out of his sight. Rolf stepped forward into the light and began the long climb up the ramp that led to the launch pad.

It was too far up the ramp to run. Rolf went as fast as the slope would let him, however, and reached the top of the pad without being seen. Being his father's son, he had absorbed enough knowledge about launchings to find his way to the primary service elevator without trouble. The primary elevator was a cage of metal bars, close-set enough so as to shield out most of the light from the floodlights without. Rolf dared not turn on the ceiling light of the elevator, which he knew was there. He groped his way to the control panel in one wall, pressed the up button and the cage rose.

He rode the elevator to the transfer point— about seventy-five feet above the surface of the pad—then left it for the narrow walkway that took him across to the secondary elevator of the launching tower. This other elevator was a more open cage, and he was able to see the pad below him as he rose. As he looked down, he saw the foreshortened figure of the first guard come back up on the level surface of the pad and look around.

Rolf gulped, but there was not time to think about the guard now. He rode the elevator to its top level, got out and crossed another narrow catwalk that led him directly to the spacecraft itself, sitting on top of the three tall sections that were the fuel-laden stages of the rocket.

He reached the spacecraft and put a hand on its smooth metal side. It's beautiful, he thought. *Like a work of art*. Now for the gremlin space kite. He reached into his hip pocket.

For a moment he thought there was nothing there, and his breath stopped in his chest. Then he felt a small papery object, and he brought it out. In the light from below, he looked at it. It was the space kite, all right, but no bigger now than the paper swan O'Rigami had folded for him when he first met the gremlin Grand Engineer.

Hardly believing that this could in fact be the kite he had seen earlier, he reached up and pressed it against the outer skin of the spacecraft.

There was something like a soundless *poof*. The tiny shape began to swell with rapidly increasing speed. In a moment it was as big as Rolf's hand, as big as a basketball, as big as . . .

The panic that had erupted in Rolf as the object suddenly began to grow in size and conspicuousness, suddenly began to die down. For the first time he noticed that as the kite got bigger, it was also getting filmier and filmier, until he could begin to see right through it . . . indeed, until it finally faded away into invisibility. Rolf stood gazing at last at a spacecraft that looked as if it had nothing attached to it at all.

So that was the secret of the space kite! He might have known the gremlins would have figured out some way to keep their space vehicle from being noticed by the human astronauts that would be boarding the metal spacecraft in the morning. He turned without wasting any more time, and hurried back to the secondary elevator to start his ride down again.

He reached the changeover point and switched to the primary elevator. This slid him downward with the noiselessness of smoothly running electrical equipment; and he had all but forgotten about the guard when it reached bottom and the door opened automatically.

"Who's that?" called a voice from the pad

just outside. "What's going on there?"

A second later the bright beam of a flashlight lanced through the open door of the elevator cage and there was the sound of running footsteps.

Rolf shrank back into a corner of the elevator, his heart thumping like the heart of a wild rabbit in a trap. If only he knew some gremlin magic—at least enough to make himself invisible. There was no way out but the open doorway of the elevator and the guard was coming straight for it. In a moment he would be discovered; and then . . .

The guard burst into the cage, actually running past Rolf.

"Who's here?" shouted the guard. "Who—"

He started to turn around. There was no chance to dodge past him without being seen. In desperation, Rolf stammered out the first thing he could think of.

"M-May the Great and Thunderous Curse of Gremla fall upon your head!" he stammered out loud.

"Wha—aaaCHOO!" exploded the guard, turning around. His flashlight wavered from floor to ceiling, out of control, as he burst into a series of gargantuan sneezes. "Who said . . . ACHooo! Ach—"

Rolf did not wait to answer him. Slipping past the blinded, sneezing man, he headed out across the pad, and down its slope toward his bicycle as the echos of body-racking sneezes floated after him through the flood-lit night.

After that narrow escape, it was almost nothing to wait for a moment when the guard on Number Twelve Gate had his back turned, and slip past him into the open freedom of the Wildlife Preserve where Shep and Baneen were waiting with the invisibility that would shield him on the road home.

10

THE launch was set for ten a.m., Eastern Daylight Time. At seven-thirty that morning, as Rolf and Rita rode their bikes out toward the Preserve, with Mr. Sheperton tagging along beside them, the roads were already crowded with carloads of people who had driven in to watch the Mars rocket's liftoff.

In the Indian and Banana rivers, small boats were anchored for the same purpose. And several miles offshore in the deep ocean water, there were even a couple of large cruise ships whose passengers had come to watch the event.

"At least the poachers won't cause any trouble," Rolf shouted to Rita as they pedaled.

"Their boat's still being repaired, thanks to Baneen."

"And how are we going to get into the Refuge?" Rita asked him. "There'll be police and security cars all over the place — it's closed up tight now."

Rolf didn't answer for a moment. He was busy shifting the rolled-up poster on the handlebars of his bike. The poster was too long to be carried safely on the rattrap behind him.

"Baneen's going to meet us halfway there and help us get there," he said at last.

"By making us invisible?" asked Rita.

With a shrug, Rolf answered, "I don't know. Gremlin magic is pretty strange. Sometimes it works fine, but just when you need it most —"

A gray sedan with official markings on its side nosed out of the traffic and started coming up toward them on the shoulder of the road. Rolf and Rita pulled their bikes aside. Rolf's heart was hammering with sudden memories of the night before. *Did the guard recognize me after all?* But the sedan went right past them; the two officers inside didn't even flick an eye at him.

With a loud "Whew!" Rolf started pedaling again.

"You know," Rita said, pulling up alongside him, "it's sort of too bad that the gremlins are going. They're kind of fun."

Rolf blinked at her. He had been thinking about something for a long time now, he realized. Just when it started to bother him, he wasn't sure. Possibly it was right after the trouble with the bulldozer out at the Hollow when both Lugh and Baneen had admitted that they didn't like people such as the boat captain who had been bringing people out to the Preserve illegally and polluting the environment. He couldn't put it into words, but something about the gremlins was nagging at him.

"You're right," he said to Rita. "I don't know if it's a good thing that they're going—"

"Good riddance to bad rubbish," Mr. Sheperton growled.

Rita still looked startled every time she heard Mr. Sheperton speak. She could accept the gremlins, but the dog's speaking always seemed to surprise her.

"Now listen Shep . . . er, Mr. Sheperton," Rolf said crossly. "I know Baneen and the others can't always be trusted to tell the exact truth, but even if they haven't been on Earth for millions of years or whatever it is, they've been around here for a long time. I wonder if maybe we don't need them?"

They were cycling past a car that had all its windows open as it inched along in the heavy traffic. A small boy's high-pitched voice piped, "He's talkin' to his doggy, Mommy. Look, he's talkin' to his doggy."

"Yes, dear," answered a woman's voice, absently. "Isn't that nice of him?"

"Need gremlins?" Rita asked as they continued along the jam-packed road. "But all they do is cause trouble. I thought they admitted that themselves."

"That's what Baneen says," Rolf admitted. "But I wonder how much of that is just showoff stuff—"

"Like diving off a high board?" Mr. Sheperton suggested drily.

"Man, can't you say anything pleasant anymore?" Rolf snapped.

"Gremlins can't be trusted," Mr. Sheperton insisted. "We need them like a flea needs flea powder. Look at what they've done to you: turned you into a thief, almost, and gotten you to sneak into the launch pad. Why, if you'd been caught—"

"Well I wasn't," said Rolf. "Not because you helped, either!"

Rita tried to nip the argument by getting back to the original subject. "If we need the gremlins the way you said we did, they must know about it, with their ability to see the future and all. So why are they leaving?"

"That's what I'd like to find out," said Rolf. "The *real* reason they're going. I've got the feeling that they've told me already, but in a very sneaky, roundabout, gremlinish sort of way. Some of the things that Lugh and Baneen had said . . . I can't seem to put my finger on exactly what it is. If I knew what it was that was really making them go, maybe I could talk them out of it."

"Talk a gremlin out of anything," muttered Mr. Sheperton, from beside Rolf's bike. "That's like talking the moon out of the sky. They're too much the experts at talking people into things, to be talked themselves. If you want to convince a gremlin of something, you've got to show him proof that is proof!"

Rolf just shook his head, feeling very confused.

"Ah, now, here we are, and a grand and lovely morning to you all," said Baneen's voice.

Rolf looked down and saw the gremlin perched on his handlebar again. This time he noticed that Baneen was sitting on the plastic handgrip of the handlebar, not on the steel itself.

"Fear not, lad," Baneen winked up at him. "None of the folks in their fume-making cars going by can see or hear me. Any more than they can hear Mr. Sheperton's grumpy old voice."

Shep growled at him.

"How long have you been there?" Rolf asked.

Baneen had turned to make horrible faces at the people in the cars they were passing. He waggled his big pointed ears, crossed his eyes, stretched out his mouth by pulling at its corners with his green fingers, and stuck out his tongue. No one noticed him at all, but several people began sneezing as they passed.

"How long have you been listening to us?" Rolf demanded.

"Why, I came as quickly as I could, overloaded as I am with duties, this glorious morn of our departure," said Baneen. "But it's true that I arrived just this moment past. Why do you ask, lad?"

"I just wondered," said Rolf.

"How are you going to get us past the patrols that are keeping people out of the Preserve?" Rita asked.

"Ah, surely that's no trouble at all," said Baneen smilingly. "Just turn in here. . . . "

They nosed their bikes off the shoulder of the road and onto the hard-packed sand. Mr. Sheperton followed them.

"And a tiny bit o' gremlin dust . . . " Baneen flung something invisible up out of his hand. The world seemed to turn into a milky white mist for a moment.

"And here we are!" Baneen said as the mist cleared.

They were indeed at the Gremlin Hollow, Rolf saw.

But things were different. For once, the hurry and scurry were missing. Little flickers and glimpses of gremlins moving about, as usual, but they seemed to be dragging along like deep-sea divers trudging on the bottom of the ocean. The glimpses Rolf caught of their small pointy faces showed them all to be wearing unusually sober, saddened expressions.

The only two completely visible were O'Rigami, who looked as imperturbable as ever, and Lugh, who stood scowling at things in general—even more blackly than usual.

Rolf got off his bike and handed the poster to O'Rigami. It was so big it nearly knocked the gremlin over.

"Ahh, many thanks," said O'Rigami, staggering slightly under the poster's weight. He bowed politely, then turned and gave the poster a flick of his hands. It floated out in midair, unrolled, and spread itself neatly on the sandy floor of the Hollow.

"Very fine," O'Rigami said. "Not precisery what we need, but crose enough."

He clapped his hands together.

"Gremrin weavers, front and center!"

There was a sort of semivisible scurry around and above the laid-out paper. Squinting at the scene, Rolf found it reminded him of how things look to someone driving through a fog—you sort of sense something is out there before you really see it.

It was impossible for any human eye to see exactly what was going on, but Rolf thought he could make out that something rather invisible was being put together on top of the poster as it lay face up. Something like the rippling of heat waves flowed across the poster from one end to the other, then slowly settled down and ceased.

"Excerrent!" said O'Rigami, to the almost-invisible gremlin workers. "Now, take firm grip."

There was evidently a good deal of effort involved in this part of the job, for a double line of gremlins flickered into visibility at both the top and bottom edges of the poster. Their tongues were clenched between their lime-colored teeth, feet planted wide, and their cheeks puffed out with effort as they clutched grimly onto something that was a good eight inches above the poster itself.

"Ready?" asked O'Rigami.

The half-visible little figures braced themselves. Suddenly, one of them at the far bottom corner of the poster lost his footing and fell. Like dominoes, the whole line along the bottom of the poster went down.

"Take care! Take care!" cried O'Rigami. "Take grip once more."

The line along the bottom of the poster formed up again.

"Now," shouted O'Rigami, "three times—as I count. Ready? *One!*"

Both lines of half-visible gremlins raised and lowered their arms. Something misty—a sheet of mistiness—formed between them, above the poster at the level where their hands were clenched.

"Two!" cried O'Rigami.

Their arms moved up and down again, accompanied by a chorus of tiny grunts and wheezes. Rolf suddenly realized that what they were doing was like what he and his friends used to do down at the beach, when they were shaking the sand off a blanket. Except that this "blanket" was a thin film of mistiness, and there was no sand on it.

"Three!" roared O'Rigami, jumping clear off the ground with his hands raised over his head.

The gremlins holding whatever-it-was flapped it once more, mightily, and fell over backward, becoming visible as they lay about looking exhausted. What they had held had also become completely visible now—it was like a thin blue veil of finest silk, shot with white. It floated downward and settled ex-

actly on top of the poster.

O'Rigami hissed with satisfaction, stepping forward to the very edge of the veil-like object.

"Why," exclaimed Rita, "it *is* a blueprint!"

In fact, what lay on the ground now, although it seemed to be made out of exquisitely fine silk, looked exactly like a very complicated technical blueprint.

"Of course," O'Rigami said to Rita. "What did you expect, a beach branket?"

"But how could you get that from the poster?" Rolf asked, staring at the blueprint.

"Now, now, lad," said Baneen abruptly. "It's as simple as enchanting a princess. The poster was made up from designs of the actual spacecraft, was it not? And since the spacecraft itself was constructed from blueprints, must it not be that the form of the blueprints was living in the design of the spacecraft, and the form of the spacecraft was living in the design of the poster? Like equals like, as one of those Greek geometers used to say. Sure and it was only the skill of the gremlin weavers it took to extract the design and make it visible."

"Oh," said Rolf, his head buzzing.

He would have said more, but now O'Rigami had just produced a small bagful of the transistors and other little items Rolf had gotten from the hardware store.

"Now," said the Grand Engineer, "we add the connectors, correctry magicked, to the brueprint, thereby energizing it and—"

He tossed the handful of small electronics components into the air. They floated out over the blueprint, descended to it, and disappeared. All but one tiny piece of red wire, which stood at one end and scurried in circles about the blueprint. O'Rigami pointed a finger and stamped his foot, the wire hopped, scooted to its proper position, and vanished with a small *poof*.

"Connection is estabrished," continued O'Rigami. "Now we attach the activated brueprints to both the human spacecraft and the space kite."

He clapped his hands. The blueprint disappeared, leaving only the poster below

it, untouched. O'Rigami turned to Lugh and bowed.

"Ready to board," he announced.

Lugh was scowling worse than ever. The look on his face would have stopped a charging bull elephant in full stride. The only good thing about it was that it did not seem to be directed at anyone in particular.

"Ready is it?" snarled Lugh. "All right then, what are the lot of you waiting for? Get on board and shake the garbage and asphalt of this miserable world from our gremlin boots!"

There was a sort of uneasy waveriness in the air of the Hollow and suddenly gremlins became visible, hundreds of them, thousands of them, all looking unhappy.

"What are you waiting for?" roared Lugh. "Did we or did we not give them their chance nearly two thousand years ago? BOARD!"

And like tiny lights going out all around Rolf, Mr. Sheperton and Rita, the hordes of gremlins began to disappear, leaving the Hollow empty with a strange and aching loneliness that Rolf could actually feel. It was a feeling such as he had never imagined before. Suddenly Lugh's last few words made sense to him, and he understood why the gremlins were really leaving Earth and why it was up to him to stop them.

"Wait!" he cried.

But all the gremlins in the Hollow were gone now except Lugh, O'Rigami and Baneen. Even as he shouted, O'Rigami gave the two humans and the dog a polite bow and disappeared. Lugh winked out almost the same instant, and Baneen thinned to transparency, flickering like a candle flame that was dying.

11

"Wait, Baneen!" Rolf shouted again, desperately.

For a second, it seemed that Baneen was almost gone. Then he grew solid again.

"Forgive me, lad," he said softly, "but I can't wait. It's time for us all to be going now, and they're waiting for me aboard the space kite. Farewell . . . "

A single tear ran down the side of his nose. He lifted a hand in a wave and began to fade again.

"Just a minute—please, Baneen—just a minute!" Rolf shouted. "Listen! I know why you're going! But you don't need to!"

"Farewell . . . " sang Baneen, mournfully.

As he grew fainter and fainter he said, "A long farewell to Earth." His tone changed abruptly and he almost smiled as he added, "And, Rolf me boy, sorry to have tricked you into helping us. It was the only way we could get away, you know."

"That's not important," Rolf insisted. "What's important is—I know why you're going! And you don't need to!"

"Ah, yes. Too bad that—you know *what*?" Baneen flickered halfway back to solid visibility.

Rolf could hardly stand still, and Rita was eyeing him in astonishment. Mr. Sheperton was sitting on his haunches, mumbling something.

"I know why you gremlins are leaving, I tell you!" said Rolf desperately. "And you don't have to! Come back, Baneen. Listen to me for just a minute!"

Baneen flickered again, faded almost completely out, then grew more and more solid until he once more stood before them as real as themselves.

"Now lad, it's no use trying to trick a gremlin. Sure, we've known all the tricks ourselves since your ancestors were painting themselves blue and hiding in caves."

"It's not a trick!" Rolf said. "I really do know why you're going back to Gremla. I would have figured it out before, but you kept telling me how you had no use for

Earth and how beautiful Gremla was. But you all really like it here on Earth, don't you?"

"Ah, what difference does it make? In less than a minute we'll be all aboard the space kite and ready for blastoff. Look—" Baneen pointed a tiny green finger. The mist of the Hollow seemed to be dissolving. Well, not exactly dissolving as much as shrinking, pulling itself together into one ball of milky whiteness that grew smaller and smaller as Rolf and the others watched it.

"You see?" Baneen said. "The magic gate is closing. I've got to get through it before it shrinks altogether and I'm stranded here while my brothers and sisters fly back to Gremla." He edged toward the shrinking sphere of whiteness.

Rolf grabbed at his skinny arm. "If you hated Earth so much, why didn't you leave centuries ago?"

Baneen looked distinctly uncomfortable. "Well, as I told you, lad, there's that dampness which keeps our magic from lifting us more than a wee distance above the ground. It's helpless we were, entirely, until you humans got the idea of building space rockets. . . ."

The milky white sphere was down to the size of a big beach ball.

"You gremlins had nothing to do with our inventing rockets?" Rolf demanded.

"Well now," said Baneen, squirming in

Rolf's grip, "maybe we did give the idea a wee push here and there. What with Mr. Da Vinci, and those Chinese fellows, and Mr. Goddard later on —"

The sphere was down to the size of a basketball. Baneen pulled, trying to get away from Rolf.

"Wait," said Rolf. "Listen to me. It was all Lugh's doing, wasn't it? All of you had come to like it here, but Lugh wasn't going to have anything to do with humans unless they were perfect, would he? He tried to make humans live up to a test that gremlins themselves couldn't even pass, nowadays. And when they couldn't do it, he decided to take you all back to Gremla—but none of you really want to go, now. You're all *Earth* gremlins—look at you, so Irish-sounding anybody'd expect to see you start sprouting shamrocks! O'Rigami, Japanese to the core! O'Kkane Baro, who's probably more gypsy than gremlin, from the way he looks to me. And La Demoiselle, who's not only so French you can't believe it, but all wound up in a bit of Earth history that won't mean a thing back on Gremla. Don't tell me, all of the rest of you really want to leave Earth! It's just Lugh! Isn't it?"

"Y-yes . . ." stammered Baneen—and clapped a hand over his mouth immediately. "What am I saying? Miscalling my own Prince—but it's true. Indeed it's true. Lugh would have it that we mustn't associate with humans unless they were able to show themselves worthy of our association. Not but what most of us have done our wee best, here and there, when the opportunity came up, little tricks to nudge your people in the right direction. But little avail it was, what with Lugh giving you a mighty push to hurry up and develop your machines and your engines, and all the rest of it, until you had something that could fly us back to Gremla as secret passengers. But how could you know about Lugh, lad?"

"Because I was the same way," Rolf said. "I was doing exactly the same thing, this last year. My mother was all wrapped up in my baby sister, and my dad had to work night and day for this launch, but I blamed them both for not being able to give me all the time they used to. I was expecting them to be perfect where I was concerned, no matter what they had to deal with anyplace else. I finally realized what I was doing, by seeing Lugh do the same thing. He's never gotten over the way it used to be back on Gremla, and he wanted Earth to be Gremla all over again. But it isn't—and he's just got to live with it, the way I have to live with my own family."

He let go of Baneen's arm, but the gremlin merely stood now, staring at him.

"Glory be!" breathed Baneen. "If Lugh could hear you—perhaps he'd change his mind yet. But—" the little gremlin wrung his hands together, "he'd never stop now, not for any simple word—"

"I'll stop him!" barked Mr. Sheperton. "I'll stop the whole pack of them, see if I don't!"

With that, the dog leaped at the magic gate.

"No!" yelped Baneen.

But Mr. Sheperton dove right through and disappeared. And the gate shriveled and shrank like a popped balloon, right behind him. As soon as Mr. Sheperton's tail flicked out of sight, the milky white sphere disappeared altogether.

"He's ruined the gate!" Baneen cried. "And he'll ruin the space kite on the other side!" Then Baneen's eyes really went wide with terror. "And how am I going to get aboard? HOW AM I GOING TO GET ABOARD?"

Rolf simply stood there, stunned. It was Rita who recovered her senses first.

"How much time do we have before the rocket takes off?" she asked.

That snapped Rolf back. He glanced at his wristwatch. "Oh no!! There's only six minutes left!"

Baneen was scampering around, distraught, pulling his eyebrows down into his mouth and chewing on them, mumbling,

"Hmlgghmmgrmll—"

Rolf grabbed him by the shoulder. "Baneen! Can you get us to the launch pad inside of six minutes?"

The gremlin shook himself. "Well I could . . . no, that wouldn't work. Or if—no, that's no good. . . ."

"Quick!" Rita said. "It's got to be right away!"

"There's only one way to do it," Baneen said, looking up at them. "But it means I'll have to go with you—and all that iron and steel—" He shuddered.

"We've got to!" Rolf insisted.

Baneen squared his shoulders. "You're right, lad. There's nothing else to do. Even though it may be the end of me, what matters one poor wee gremlin when—"

"Can it!" Rita shouted. "Let's get going!"

"Right!" cried Baneen. "Onto your bikes, you two." And he glided up and sat on Rolf's handlebar.

The bikes?" Rita asked.

"We've only got five minutes," said Rolf.

"Trust me," said Baneen, with an almost saintly smile on his gremlin face.

It wasn't like any bike ride in the history of the world. The instant their feet touched the pedals, the bicycles took off like racing cars and went faster and faster. The bush and sand dunes went blurring past.

"There's the road now!" Baneen yelled over the howling wind. He was hanging onto the plastic handgrip of the handlebar with one tiny hand, and keeping his hat jammed on his head with the other. "Follow it in to the base!"

They were going at least seventy miles an hour, Rolf guessed—and straight toward the double line of cars that still jammed the road.

"We'll crash," cried Rolf, as he squeezed the handbrakes. But the brakes didn't slow the bike at all. He and Rita—with Baneen hanging on by one hand—hurtled directly at the traffic on the road.

12

For one instant it seemed they were going to
smash right into the side of a big mobile
home. Then the handlebars twitched by
themselves, and suddenly both bikes were
weaving in and out among the cars and
trailers and campers, zooming along the road
at fantastic speed, the wind screeching past
so fast that Rolf could scarcely breathe.

Frantic drivers jammed on their brakes.
Children and mothers sat staring, pop-eyed,
as the two bikes roared past them at the
speed of jet planes. Half the time Rolf simply closed his eyes as they scooted between
cars, around trucks, and—he swore—*over* a
busload of tourists from Dayton, Ohio.

Baneen had slipped off the handgrip and was flapping in the wind, hanging on with one hand and screaming madly.

"Ouch! Oh! All this—oof!—iron and steel! Ouch! Great Gremla protect me—ouch!"

Behind them the cars they passed set up a honking, like a mechanical chorus of angry machines. They zipped past a checkpoint, and the guard standing beside his gray sedan let the radio microphone drop from his hand as he stared at the two nearly supersonic bikes roaring by. His partner picked up the microphone and started babbling into it.

They passed the entrance to the Space Center so fast that the guards there were knocked down by the blast of wind. They scrambled to their feet and started yelling into their microphones:

"Two bicycles—must be doing five-hundred miles an hour—yeah, yeah, *bicycles*! No, I don't have sunstroke!"

Back at the Manned Launch Center, Rita's father shook his head at the hastily typed report that had just been handed to him. Security guards were bustling around the room he was in, other men and women were sitting at radio desks and working typewriters.

Mr. Amaro's eyes widened as he read the report. "Five-hundred miles an hour? Bicycles? Are they all going crazy out there?"

An excited voice came through one of the

radio loudspeakers: "I can see 'em! They're a couple of kids—the bikes are goin' so fast they're just a blur. And they're headin' straight for the VAB!"

Mr. Amaro crumpled the typewritten sheet in his hand. "Crazy or not, nobody's getting into the Vehicle Assembly Building without a pass! Come on."

Meanwhile Rolf and Rita were zooming along, heading for the enormous, massive shape of the VAB, where the rockets are put together before they are taken out to their launch pads.

"Ouch! Oh! Will we never get there?" Baneen was groaning.

"Look!" Rita yelled over the howling wind. "Security cars coming!"

Rolf saw the white cars speeding toward

them from both sides of the VAB. "We can't go around!" he shouted. "They've got both sides blocked!"

"Do something!" Rita yelled to Baneen.

"All right—owoo!" cried Baneen. "Straight up, then—ooch, ouch! The whole building's full of iron, isn't it?"

They hurtled directly at the straight solid wall of the VAB as if they were going to smash themselves against it. Rolf involuntarily closed his eyes, and the next thing he knew their bikes were racing straight *up* the wall, defying gravity and going as fast as ever.

Down at the base of the building, Mr. Amaro hopped out of his car before the driver had even brought it to a complete stop. He snapped his head back so fast that his uniform cap fell off.

"I don't believe it!" he muttered to himself. "I see it, but it's impossible!"

The two bikes went right up to the top of the wall and disappeared over the edge of the roof.

"It's like being on top of a mountain," Rolf yelled as they bounced onto the roof of the VAB. "This is the highest point in all Florida, I bet."

"It's nice being away from all those horns and the people yelling," Rita agreed.

But they only had a moment to enjoy the quiet and the view. With Baneen still *ouch*ing every inch of the way, they hurtled straight for the far edge of the roof.

Rolf felt his stomach drop away as his bike—and Rita's—raced right off the roof and did a "Wheelie" on the back wall of the VAB. They both sailed down the wall with only their rear wheels touching. Rolf squinted downward. There was nothing between his madly pedaling feet and the ground except hundreds of feet of very thin air.

"Don't look down!" he yelled to Rita, as his hands suddenly went clammy.

"Why not?" Rita hollered back. "It's fun! Man, is that a long way down!"

Rolf concentrated on keeping his teeth from chattering.

They got to the ground and scooted off again, just as a couple of security cars pulled around the corner of the building.

"Whew," said Baneen, pulling himself back up to a sitting position. "At least we're away from that nasty iron for a moment or two."

Rolf glanced at his wristwatch. Two minutes to go before liftoff.

They were heading straight for the giant rocket and its launch stand, with a half dozen white security cars trailing along behind them, sirens blaring distantly. But now Rolf saw that between them and the launch stand were more cars, and hundreds of people sitting in the press stands.

"How can we get around them?" he

asked Baneen.

"Not around," puffed Baneen. "Over." Then the gremlin asked in a lower, sadder tone, "By the way, lad, that launching stand and the great tall tower — they're made of iron, aren't they?"

"Steel," said Rolf.

Baneen's eyes rolled up and the corners of his mouth dropped. "Ah, well — up and away!"

The bicycles soared into the air for a short distance, then bounced back to the ground. Another hop, longer this time, took them over a row of parked cars. Baneen winced and fidgeted. Then they bounded over a startled group of photographers, who jumped and shouted, and knocked over each others' tripods in their surprise.

Bouncing, they reached the press stands where the reporters and photographers were eagerly watching the final moments of countdown. They soared over the watchers, who yelled and ducked as the bikes cleared their heads by inches.

They bounced down on the apron of ground between the viewing stand and the canal of water that ran between the launch stand and the VAB.

"Water!" screeched Baneen. "Merciful Gremla!"

The canal was about two hundred yards across, and deep, as Rolf knew. And they were hurtling for it too fast to swerve aside.

"Up and over!" shouted Baneen, his voice quavering.

The two bicycles soared up like gliders and rose over the canal. Baneen put a hand over his eyes while he wailed, "Water . . . oo!"

Rolf also closed his eyes. He didn't mind flying in a plane, but in a bicycle . . . !

He felt his bike touch down again, but on something that wasn't quite solid ground. Opening his eyes, Rolf saw that they were pedaling up a wire, with Rita's bike right in front of him. Like circus acrobats, they raced up the steeply angled wire.

Pushing down a lump in his throat, Rolf shouted ahead to Rita, "This is the escape wire—the astronauts use this to slide down from the spacecraft in case something goes wrong right before the rocket ignites."

Rita half-turned in her seat to look at him over her shoulder. "I know. Isn't it fun?" She was grinning broadly.

Fun! Rolf felt paralyzed as they raced up the slim strand of wire, and she thought it was fun. *She's got more faith in gremlin magic than I have!*

Meanwhile, more than a dozen white security cars had pulled up to a screaming halt beside the launch pad.

Half a dozen guards ran over to Mr. Amaro's car. He jumped out and started shouting to them:

"Well, where are they? Have you seen them?"

"No, sir. Can't find them anywhere!" None of the men was looking high enough to see the two bicycles zooming up the escape wire. The bikes were just a blur anyway; they were going so fast.

"Well, spread out," Mr. Amaro ordered. "They must have sneaked in among the crowd someplace."

One of the guards, his face sweaty and worried-looking, asked, "Sir, should we ask Mission Control to put a hold on the countdown? Those kids might be anyplace—"

"No," Mr. Amaro said. "they've got awfully fast motorbikes, I'll admit. But they'd have to be able to fly to get across the canal and into the launch area itself. There's no chance of that."

"Right," the other guard agreed.

Up, up and up the two bikes raced while Baneen shuddered and moaned. "Iron and steel, iron and steel. Ooohhh."

Finally they thumped to a stop, and Rolf saw that they were now on the same platform he had come to the night before, in the elevator. The spacecraft was standing at one end of the platform, smooth and white. The space kite itself was hanging from the spacecraft's outer skin, looking tiny and barely visible—but at the same time, Rolf thought it looked big as a jetliner. He could see thousands of gremlins jostling around inside the kite, flickering in and out of visibility like a set of winking Christmas lights.

Somewhere a loudspeaker was saying, "Thirty seconds and counting. . . . The launch tower is now starting to roll away from the rocket vehicle and spacecraft."

And the tower was beginning a slow, grinding, growling motion.

"Lugh, ye great hulking heap of princely magic!" Baneen cried out, hopping on the steel platform as if it were covered with hot coals. "Come . . . oooch! . . . quick. There's grand news!"

"Twenty seconds and counting . . ."

Lugh appeared at the edge of the kite, as if he were standing on a wing of it. "What is it now, trickster? Are you staying with the humans, after all?"

"Listen — ouch! — quick, Lugh me darling. There's no need to leave Earth. None at all. For any of us!"

Before Lugh could reply, though, Rolf broke in, "Where's Shep — Mr. Sheperton?"

"Ten seconds, nine, . . . "

"The dog?" Lugh scowled. "Tried to rip our kite off the rocket, he did. I cooled him off. Down there!"

Lugh pointed, turned his back and walked off toward the edge of the platform. Rolf stared down in the direction the other had indicated and saw Mr. Sheperton paddling weakly in a large pond of water.

That's the water that feeds into the exhaust cooling sprays! Rolf realized. *In a few seconds the pumps will suck Shep down and then fire him right into the hot exhaust gases when the rocket takes off!*

"Nine, eight . . . "

"Stop the launch!" Rolf yelled. Desperately, he looked about him. Lugh still stood with his back turned. Then a glitter caught Rolf's eye. The Great Corkscrew of Gremla was taking form beside him. He glanced at it, and saw standing behind it O'Rigami, La Demoiselle, and O'Kkane Baro, along with other gremlins whose names he did not know. The voice of Baneen whispered in his ear.

"Pull it out, lad—quickly. We'll help!"

Already, O'Rigami and the others were disappearing into the glitter of the case of the Great Corkscrew. Frantically, Rolf took hold and pulled. There was a moment when nothing happened and then suddenly the Great Corkscrew slid easily from its case and the brilliant light flashing from it glittered all around. Lugh spun about.

"Stop the launch!" shouted Rolf, holding the Corkscrew aloft and waving it at the gremlin prince.

"Five . . . four . . . " boomed the loudspeaker. Lugh stood, staring.

Rolf could not wait any longer for Lugh to

act. He threw the Corkscrew aside, and dived for the hook at the end of the escape wire. In an eyeblink he was sliding madly back *down* the wire, racing toward the ground and the water at the edge of the launch pad, nothing between him and a five-hundred-foot fall except the strength of his fingers as they clutched the hook of the handgrip.

The loudspeaker droned. "Two, one . . . zero . . ."

Rolf's feet touched the ground and he ran pell-mell to the edge of the tank and without an instant's hesitation, dived in. Mr. Sheperton was still struggling in the water as if some invisible force were binding his legs.

"Shep, Shep—I'm here! I'll save you!" Rolf yelled as he swam toward the dog.

"Too late . . ." gargled Mr. Sheperton, weakly, and his head sank beneath the surface of the water.

In the Launch Control room—a place filled with technicians and engineers sitting at row after row of control consoles—Mr. Gunnarson snapped a ballpoint pen in half and threw the pieces on the floor beside his desk.

"No ignition! The rockets didn't light off!" A half dozen men huddled around him.

"Must be the firing sequencer."

"Or the main squib."

"Or a pump failure."

Mr. Gunnarson wanted to slam the desk with both his fists. Instead, he swallowed hard and said as calmly as he could,

"Are there any malfunction lights showing on the consoles?"

"No, everything's green."

He took a deep breath. "All right. Set the countdown sequencer back to T minus two minutes and go through it again. Maybe we've just got a loose connection. Tell the astronauts that we're recycling to T minus two—and counting!"

"Right!" The men scurried back to their consoles.

Mr. Amaro appeared at Mr. Gunnarson's elbow. "There's been some funny kind of disturbance around the pad—a couple of kids on motorcycles. . . . "

"Not now!" Mr. Gunnarson snapped. "We've got a bird loaded and ready to go. Like a live bomb out there!"

One instant Rolf was diving under the water to grab at Shep's sinking form, and the next instant he was standing in the middle of the Gremlin Hollow, dripping wet, with Shep beside him.

"What the—"

Shep shook himself, and a shower of water sprayed from his soaked fur. "Hey, wait, cut it out!" Rolf yelled, trying to protect himself with his hands.

He rubbed the water from his eyes and felt the hot Florida sun baking him dry. Then the air of the Hollow shimmered and Rita appeared, holding both their bicycles, looking rather surprised and troubled.

"Rolf, you're all right!"

"Yeah, sure . . . but . . . "

Suddenly the air about them was filled with fireflies, thousands of dancing lights that spun around their heads and settled to the ground. Wherever one of the sparkling lights touched down, it turned into a gremlin. And now the gremlins were laughing and dancing lightly, grabbing each other and whirling around, arm in arm. Baneen was dancing with La Demoiselle. O'Rigami was twirling with O'Kkane Baro.

Lugh appeared, and he was neither laughing nor dancing. Rolf had never seen the gremlin leader look more grim or more terrible. At the sight of their prince, the other gremlins stopped dancing and their laughter faded into silence.

"So!" said Lugh, looking up at Rolf and at the same time seeming to tower mountainously over him. "You'd trick a gremlin would you—you'd try to pull the wool over the eyes of Lugh of the Long Hand? Well, it's a short delay you'll find you'll have gained, in a moment—and a long time of sorrow to repent interfering with our departure! So, you bid me stop the launch by virtue of the Great Wish gained when you drew our Corkscrew from its case, did you? I suppose you'll not be shy about drawing the Corkscrew forth once more, just to show me while my eyes are on you, how the strength to do so is in you, and you alone?"

"I . . ."

"Ah, now, Lugh!" chattered Baneen, appearing beside Rolf with O'Rigami and the rest. "Sure, and it's a terrible hard thing to do, drawing the Great Corkscrew from its holding place. You wouldn't be requiring the lad to do it more than once, and that second time right on the heels of his first mighty effort. How much better to admit ourselves beaten—"

"SILENCE!" roared Lugh. Silence fell over the Hollow. "BOY, LET ME SEE YOU DRAW THE CORKSCREW FORTH!"

The Great Corkscrew, once more in its case, winked into existence in front of Rolf. Half-paralyzed by Lugh's voice, he reached out and took hold of it, pulling at it. And then, a strange thing began to happen . . .

In front of Rolf's eyes . . . in front of Lugh, himself . . . first Baneen, and then, one by one, O'Rigami, La Demoiselle, and O'Kkane Baro, along with other nameless gremlins, began once more to disappear into the glare and glitter of the case . . . and the Corkscrew once more came forth in Rolf's hand.

Lugh stared. For a second his jaw worked,

but no sound came out. Then, incredulously, he spoke.

"What . . . what *is* this? MUTINY?"

Baneen and the others reappeared.

"Ah, Lugh, darling!" cried the little gremlin. "Sure, and we'd never go against your wishes, ordinarily. But it's fond of this world we are, to be sure, after all these thousands of years, and—"

"Silence!" thundered Lugh. "What kind of gremlins are you?"

"We are ze good gremlins!" cried La Demoiselle. "Eet ees because we are true gremlins zat we fight to stay on ze Earth!"

"FIGHT?" roared Lugh. "Well the lot of you know that it's myself alone—" he shook one knobby fist, "is more than a match for all of you put together. What, must I take you all up under my arm and carry you back to Gremla by force? If so be it, I will—"

He began to roll up his sleeves.

"Wait!" shouted Rolf. Lugh paused and looked at him. "Wait," Rolf said again, more quietly. "This is my fault, but somebody's got to tell you you're wrong—"

"Silence, human!" rumbled Lugh ominously, continuing to roll up his sleeves.

"I'm not going to be silent," said Rolf. "You're just like I was—"

Lugh paused in rolling his sleeves, and stared at Rolf in astonishment.

"I?" he said. "Lugh of the Long Hand,

like a mere human-lad?"

"That's right," said Rolf, determined now to get the words said, no matter how Lugh would react to them. "I kept trying to make my parents be the way I wanted them, in spite of the fact that they had other responsibilities. And you've been trying to turn Earth into another Gremla—into Gremla all over again, with the drawing of the Great Corkscrew and someone being king, and all that—and now that it hasn't worked, you're going to run away, back to Gremla and Hamrod the Heartless. Even Hamrod's better than admitting you were wrong!"

Lugh's ears rotated slowly, twice.

"Do I hear what I think I hear?" he muttered. "A human, saying such to *me*?"

"It's time somebody said it to you!" Rolf shouted. "None of the other gremlins want to go back to Hamrod. They've come to love Earth—and so have you, only you won't admit it! If you'd admit it to yourself, you'd be willing to work with humans, even if none of them has a big enough soul to draw the Great Corkscrew from its case without help, any more than there's any gremlin who can. Can *you* pull the Great Corkscrew loose by yourself? Of course not! So what makes you the one to decide whether all the gremlins on Earth have to go back to Gremla?"

Lugh began to swell . . . his actual body began to enlarge until he seemed to be growing to twice his normal size. As for his aura, that large impression that hovered over him at all times, it grew and grew until it seemed as large as a mountain. He spoke—and his voice was so deep that it seemed to come from the bowels of the earth and shake the very Hollow around them like an earthquake.

"L I G H T N I N G!" said Lugh, in that awful voice.

Suddenly the sky was black with clouds over their heads. A roll of thunder rumbled, echoing the sound of Lugh's voice and a jagged spear of lightning shot down from the clouds and was caught, still jagged and so bright none of them could look at it, in Lugh's right hand.

He poised the shaft of lightning, aiming it toward Rolf.

"B O Y!" he said. "A D M I T Y O U L I E!"

Wincing away from the blinding glare of the lightning shaft burning in Lugh's hand, Rolf shook his head stubbornly.

"No!" he cried. "I'm right! You're the one who's wrong!"

For a moment there was a terrible hush in the Hollow. Lugh stood still. Then he lifted his arm.

Suddenly the lightning shaft flew from his hand back up to the clouds. The clouds themselves rolled up and disappeared. Bright sunshine poured down again on them all;

and a great sigh of relief went up from thousands of gremlin throats.

"Ah, sure, your honor!" piped the voice of Baneen. "And wasn't it yourself said that if you could find a human who cared more for another creature than himself, you'd give that human the Great Wish? And haven't we here a lad who today risked everything, his own life included, for that of his faithful dog — and sure, if a dog's not a creature now, what is?"

Lugh stared fiercely at Baneen, and then at Rolf, and then off into the distance.

"Quick, lad!" whispered Baneen in Rolf's ear. "Make your wish — *now*!"

"I wish," said Rolf, rapidly, "that gremlins would work with humans from now on to clean up the world and keep it clean and safe!"

"There, Lugh, darling!" cried Baneen, dancing in front of the gremlin prince. "It was yourself heard his wish. Do you grant it, now?"

Lugh glared at Baneen and turned to glare again at Rolf.

"Harrumph!" he growled, deep in his throat. "*Rahumpf!* HAHR-rumphff . . . all right!"

He turned and stalked off. The gremlins in the Hollow burst into wild cheering.

Abruptly, the ground shook. The air vibrated as if some giant's breath were roaring across the world. And off in the distance, as wave after wave of thunder rolled across the Hollow, they all saw the Mars rocket lifting up, up, climbing straight into the cloudless blue sky on a tongue of sheer flame.

"A beautifur feat of engineering," Rolf heard O'Rigami say.

The Mars rocket climbed higher, the roar of its mighty engines diminished. It became a distant speck, then a bright, fast-moving star shining in the morning sky. Then it got so far away that none of them could see it any longer.

Rolf felt as if he wanted to cheer, but it was all too magnificent and overpowering for something as small as one human voice. But it really did not matter. The gremlins were all cheering, for him. Rita was trying to hug him. The gremlins nearby were trying to hug him. Mr. Sheperton was standing on his hind legs, trying to lick Rolf's face. It was all sort of a wonderful mess.

13

" . . . Crazy, the whole business," said Rolf's father, thoughtfully. "Absolutely crazy! On the other hand, does it matter? The bird got off all right, with only that short two-minute hold at the last minute—"

"What caused that?" asked Rolf's mother. "You didn't tell me."

"One of those one-in-a-million things," Rolf's father dismissed the hold with a wave of his hand. "A loose connection in the ignition wiring. When we recycled and tried again, the light was white and there was no evidence that it had ever been anything else. But I'm not talking about that. . . . "

Rolf fidgeted in his chair at the breakfast

table. Rita, he knew, would be waiting at her place for him, by this time, but he dared not call attention to himself by leaving the table. His father, like most generally easygoing men, had one or two crotchets. One of them was that the whole family should be together at the breakfast table.

" . . . We never see each other the rest of the time," he was in the habit of saying. "The least we can do is sit down and have a decent breakfast together before the day starts."

All of which, of course, did not mean that Rolf could not leave the table—but he would bother his father by doing so, and his father's reaction, when bothered, was suddenly to start remembering all the questions he normally did not get around to asking Rolf, such as where he was all day yesterday, and why didn't he use his dependent's pass to watch the rocket launch, and what had he been doing lately anyway? Rolf could lose more time than he would just sitting and waiting for his father to remember it was time to go to the office.

" . . . Almost enough to make you believe in gremlins," his father was saying.

"Gremlins?" Rolf's mother asked, trying to get a spoonful of applesauce into the baby without half of it going on to the flowered bib around the baby's neck.

"Gremlins—imaginary little troublemakers

that are always keeping things from working right," said Rolf's Dad with another wave. "Someone dreamed them up during World War II, I think. I didn't mean it seriously about believing in them. Not that there aren't all kinds of things . . . "

His mind wandered.

"What things, dear?" asked Rolf's mother, wiping the baby's chin with the bib.

"Well, that business the guards reported about some people on motorcycles running all over the place."

"Did they find them?" Rolf's mother asked. "The checkout girl in the supermarket was saying . . . "

Rolf's dad snorted. He sounded almost like Shep.

"I've heard the rumors!" he said. "Bicycles riding at a hundred ninety miles an hour up one side of the VAB and down the other? Bicycles bouncing all over the Press Stand? Ridiculous. Besides, if there was anyone actually involved in something like that, how would they have gotten out of the Space Center, with every security man and car on duty looking for them?

"Well, at least everything's A-okay with the spacecraft. The astronauts have been reporting that everything's working absolutely perfectly. No gremlins aboard the spacecraft!"

Rolf struggled to keep a straight face.

Mr. Gunnarson sneezed.

"Are you catching a cold?" demanded Rolf's mother, looking suddenly at him.

"No . . . no, I don't think so," said Rolf's father. "Just thinking about that sneezing fit everybody had out at the launch a minute or two after the hold was called. No one knows about that either. There's a notion that some unusual cloud of pollen blew in about that time. Well, there you are. Things all over the place not making sense—"

He gestured at the newspaper he had just laid down.

"Half a dozen U.S. senators opposed to the Wildlife Reclamation bill got caught in an elevator that stuck between floors and missed their chance to vote against the bill. It passed," he said. "Some boat owner who'd been sneaking people into the Playalinda Beach area to watch launches ran it up on the beach there and was stranded. Got caught. Claimed he was going into a canal a friend of his had made months before—only somebody had moved the canal. Nonsense! Actually, he'd missed the canal entrance by a good fifty yards. Must have been blind. Then, here, it says that it looks as if the Space Program's going to get a financial shot in the arm so that the Space Lab can get to work on wider-ranging studies of how to combat air pollution and topsoil erosion while surveying for more deposits of natural resources."

"Wasn't the Space Lab doing a lot of that sort of thing anyway?" Rolf's mother asked, lifting Rolf's baby sister out of her highchair.

"Of course. Amazing how few people seemed to know about it though," Rolf's dad answered. "Still, this is going to make that part of the work here a lot more important. Which reminds me — the surprise I mentioned I'd have for you after the launch. I've been asked if I want to shift into this new ecological study work."

"You?" said Rolf, staring at him.

"Yes. It's been a pet project of mine for some time. I didn't want to say anything to you both because I wasn't sure it could be pushed through. But it's all set now. I'd be Engineering Director for it," said Mr. Gunnarson, thoughtfully. "It means I'd have to go running off on trips to various parts of the world from time to time, but maybe we could tie some of those trips in with family vacations."

"Why, I think it's marvelous!" said Rolf's mother. "Why didn't you tell me until now?"

"Well, you were asleep when I came in at four a.m. after we got the launch wrapped up," said Rolf's father. "Besides, the only time this family ever gets together is at breakfast, and I thought we'd all talk about it together."

He looked at Rolf, who was staring back at him.

"What do you think, Rolf?" he asked. Rolf gulped.

"Cool!" he said, hastily, getting up from the table. "But I've got to go now. Rita's waiting for me."

"Rita. That's nice," said his mother. "I'm so glad to see you spending some time with your friends for a change."

"By the way, you didn't ask me for a dependent's pass to the launch," said Rolf's father. "Where were you yesterday?"

"Oh, just around," said Rolf, halfway out the door.

"And come to think of it," said his father, "weren't you asking about a ten-speed bike back there a week or so ago?"

"Uh . . . well," Rolf edged back toward the kitchen door. "I guess my old three-speed is fast enough, Dad. Really."

"But . . ."

"I've got to go!" Rolf slipped out the kitchen door and paused only briefly in the hall to grab a towel from the linen closet.

"Where are you going, dear?" called his mother.

"Swimming! Down at the pool!" Rolf shouted back, stepping out the back door. His bike was waiting there with his bathing suit already in the rattrap. He added the towel to it and climbed on. *Wait,* he thought, *until I tell Rita. . . .*

"I thought—" A shadow that was his dad's

face spoke to him through the curtains of the half-open kitchen window, "you said you couldn't swim because your leg bothered you—"

"Oh, my leg's fine!" Rolf called back. "It's been fine for weeks. See you!"

He cycled off.

"That boy . . . " he heard his father beginning behind him; but the rest of the words were left behind. Rolf wheeled down the street in the morning sunlight; and for a second his father's words about the new job and family vacation came back to him. His father—of all people! He felt sharply uncomfortable for a second, thinking how he had misjudged his dad. Then, the uncomfortableness was washed away by the thought of the trips. It really would be cool zipping around the world. Wait until he told Rita, and the other kids at school. He would have to ask Baneen how to go about finding the local gremlins in other places, once he got there. He wondered if the dogs in Spain or Japan spoke Spanish or Japanese, or whether he would be able to understand them the way he was still able to understand Shep. . . .

No point in letting the fact that he could see gremlins and talk to animals go to waste.

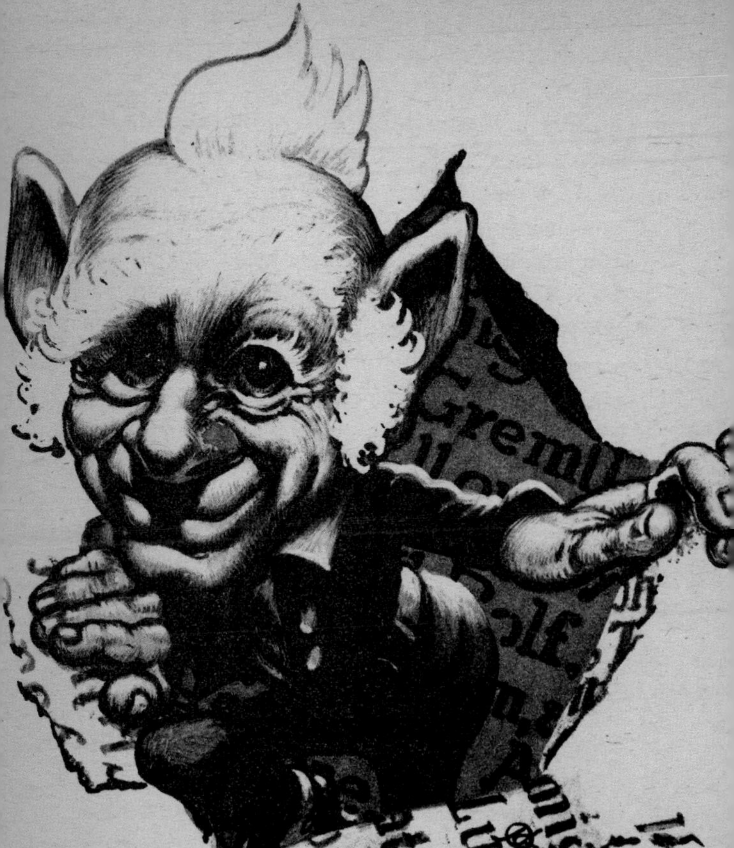